I'M HIS QUEEN, HE'S MY KING

PERK THIRTY

Cale Hart
LITERATURE NOVELS

I'm His Queen, He's My King

Mailing List

To stay up to date on new releases, plus get information on contests, sneak peeks, and more,

Go To The Website Below...

www.colehartsignature.com

PREFACE

The game of Chess is the most strategic and mind-boggling game ever created.

The goal? Keep the King from being checkmated, and you win the game.

There are many pieces that fight on the front line to protect the King. Everyone wants to overthrow him and covet his position and power. Many plot and come for the throne, but only those who have what it takes will succeed.

The beautiful thing about Chess, is it involves the most important piece on the board. The one piece that can go wherever she pleases and make the moves she makes in order to protect her **King**. That one piece in the game has more power than any other player...

I

QUEEN

DECEMBER 31, 2019

I was fitted to death for me and my homegirls New Year's party. I splurged on a purple Dolce & Gabbana dress, matching six-inch stilettos, and a purse that was waaaay over my budget. But fuck it, 2020 was about to be the year of clear vision! New goals, new moves, and new heights were the *only* things I was trying to see.

I broke up with my ex on Thanksgiving. That mofo was seeing not one, not two, but *three* bitches on the side, and had the nerve to tell me he loved me. *Hmpf!* Love my ass! I was in "all men are dogs" mode from that point on. And I was *not* getting into a relationship anytime soon.

For the New Year, me and my friends pitched in on a Chalet swimming pool suite at the Sybaris. That room was *dope!* It had a full-size swimming pool on the first floor of the suite. A twelve-foot waterslide went from the second-floor master bedroom loft into the swimming pool. There was a misting steam room, fireplace, hottub jacuzzi in one of the bedrooms, massage chair, and big fluffy robes and slippers that felt like velvet marshmallows.

"Shiiid, look at this, girl," my best friend Jenny commented.

She was pointing to the mirror on the ceiling. She flicked some lights on and off, and stars appeared on the mirror, making tiny constellations dance on the bedsheets. "Bullshit ain't nothin.' I'm getting me some on *this* tonight!" She laughed and plopped down on the huge bed.

"Ugh, you nasty, girl," my friend Sarah said. It was four of us. We had the suite, the drinks, the smoke, and plenty of adult games like *Drunk, Stoned, Or Stupid, Cards Against Humanity, If You Had To...* and *XXX Charades.* The plan was to bring in the New Year with a **BANG!**

I was trying to get drunk, chill in the hot tub, and watch the ball drop. I wasn't big on smoking like a couple of the girls, but I'd take a few celebratory puffs to bring in 2020. Hopefully the "gas" they had wouldn't make me paranoid or throw-up - two side effects that had been known to plague me damn near every time I got high. I knew some men would be showing up at some point, and I didn't want to make a fool of myself by being *too* fucked up.

I took a grand tour of our pimpish ass pool suite and smiled to myself. Life wasn't so bad. I was saving a lot of money because of all the OT I put in toward the end of the year. I took on every available bonus shift just to work and keep my mind off of my bad break-up with Devontae. That nigga didn't just break my heart; he put a hole in my *soul.* I was discombobulated mentally because my confidence was all fucked up. I mean, I wasn't a sedity chick, but I did know that I was an attractive woman. So when I saw the ratchet ass bitches he cheated on me with, I was like, *Really? You're into trifling ass, busted-up bitches over someone who has their shit together?* But that's a dog for ya. He doesn't give a fuck what he humps on. As long as he could get on it how he wants to, do his thang, and run off when he's done with his amusement. *Woof woof* right? *SMH.*

But I wasn't sweating no men. *If someone caught my eye, maybe I'd have some fun*, I said to myself and shrugged. The night was still young.

I played with the light switches, flicking them on and off, trying to learn which buttons were for what part of the suite. I was having a hard time sitting because my vagina was throbbing like crazy. I hadn't had sex in months, and my favorite vibrator broke weeks ago, so I figured my "pussy problems" were from a lack of sexual healing. I knew I'd have to do something about it sooner or later, so if Marvin Gaye came on, the panties would be coming *off*. That constant throb that wouldn't leave me alone would then be quenched.

I went into each bedroom and admired the beautiful décor. Each room had its own jacuzzi next to the bed, a lounge area in the corner underneath a fireplace, a massage chair, and an all-marble bathroom. It even had one of those fancy toilets they had in Europe where the water sprays up your business and cleans you up.

I laid on my bed and looked at myself in the mirror. *This some freaky ass shit*, I thought to myself. The suite was meant for sex and partying. Three feet from my bed was a jacuzzi big enough to fit ten people in. A mirrored ceiling was over my bed, and a fireplace was in the corner. It cost a pretty penny just for one night, but then again, there was only one New Year's Eve 2020 night. We were definitely going to turn up!

Before joining the girls, I decided to try the bidet for the first time. It took a minute to figure out how it worked, but the cold water shooting up my genitals was a refreshing feeling. It was weird at first, but I could see why rich people had that kind of stuff in their homes. It felt *gooood*. It hurt to wipe my throbbing vagina, so the bidet toilet was a welcomed addition for me.

When I exited the bathroom, I could hear them. We brought two bass speakers, and the music was thumping so loud I could feel my heart rattle inside of my chest!

"Ay! Ay! Ay! Ay!" the girls chanted as they danced on the bed.

"Alright, bitches, where's my drink?" I announced over the music.

"Right here girrrrl!" Jenny announced, pulling the gallon of

Crown Royal Apple out of the cooler. I looked at the frosty bottle, ice cold and calling my name.

"A'ight then, pass that shit. You know a Queen-"

"Must have her Crown!" My friends chanted with me.

I tore off the plastic wrapping and twisted the gold crown off the top. I was passed two glasses. One for me and one for Nikki. She was the only one of my girls who drank Crown. Jenny was into vodka, and Sarah liked her Patrón. Mixing white and brown with them was a wild risk. So they each had their own bottle.

Everyone had a full glass and I raised mine high in the air. "2020 vision y'all. In four hours, we're getting on some new shit. Set them goals and follow them through until we see them in person. 2019 was shit, but we're gonna make 2020 sweet. 2020 is our year!"

"2020 is our year!" my friends repeated. We clinked glasses and gulped down our liquor straight, no chaser.

Hours later, I was feeling no pain. The men arrived, and they brought more weed and liquor, amongst other things.

"Yo, you fuck with the rollers, ma?" a light-skinned dude named Skinny said. He was alright looking, but not my type. He had so many face tattoos it was hard to look him in the eyes. My homegirls invited a bunch of men they met on Snapchat and Facebook.

"The who?" I asked in my own fog. He pulled out a bag of colorful pills and placed a few of them in his palm.

"Rollers. Beans. X. Molly."

"Ohhhh, that's Molly?" I asked, picking up the pills and investigating them. One was in the shape of the superman sign. It was blue with pink swirls throughout the Skittles-sized pill. Another one was a Transformer head, but the one that caught my eye was the big, pink Hello Kitty pill. My childhood idol was before my eyes in the form of a pretty "party" pill.

"So this is what all the rappers be talking about when they say Molly huh? What does it do to you?"

"It makes you feel gooooood, babygirl." Skinny cooed in my ear.

"It's not laced with no bullshit that's gon fuck my brain up is it?" I asked seriously. He burst out laughing and I got up and walked away.

"Hey ma, hold up!" ol' boy screamed after me. I paid him no mind as I walked back into the party. There were a few dudes I thought were cute, but Skinny was the only one to approach me. I agreed to go somewhere quiet to let him shoot his shot, but he missed.

On some bold ass Queen shit, I walked up to a chocolate brother who had his own gallon bottle of Crown Royal Peach. I took the bottle out of his hand, sat on his lap, popped the Hello Kitty pill in my mouth, and washed it down with Crown.

"Oh, so that's how it's gon' be?" Skinny asked, standing over us.

"Looks like the lady chose up, fam," the guy whose lap I was sitting on said. Skinny sulked off with his tail between his legs.

"Thank you," I said.

"No problem, ma. I saw you when I first stepped in. I thought fa sho' you was spoken for, so I didn't holla," he said. I looked at him through beer goggles. He wasn't bad looking, but I was definitely seeing two of him. My vagina throbbed harder and harder. I knew I was going to give him some and never see him again, and that was fine by me. It was 11:27, and I wanted to bring in the New Year with a BANG!

"Look, I don't know what your name is, and I don't care what your name is. When the clock strikes twelve, I want to be getting my pussy ate like a Queen. Do it good, and you can have your way with me. You down?" I asked and sucked his earlobe.

"Say less," the strong man said as he stood up with me in his arms. I ran my fingers through his dreads and wrapped my legs around his waist like a belt. When I looped my hands around his neck, he casually walked with me hanging on to him into my room. I jumped down and kicked my shoes off. He did the same.

I walked over to the jacuzzi and began filling it with hot water. I threw a few bath bombs in and slipped out of my dress. He took a swig from his Crown bottle and extended it to me.

I walked up to him in my lace bra and panty set. He unbuttoned his shirt and threw it on the bed. I tilted my head back while he held the bottle over my face. I opened my mouth and he poured in the warm, brown liquor. The strong whiskey coated my throat with a burst of heat, leaving behind a pleasant peach aftertaste.

By 11:50, I was on the edge of the jacuzzi getting a tongue bath by the handsome chocolate man. "Ohhh, yes! Get in that muthafucka baby. Suck the nectar out of my sweet juicy peach. You like peach so much...mmmm, drink this." I gasped and grabbed the back of his head. I pushed his face into my vagina and smothered him with my Queendom. My orgasm was building, but I wanted to cum at midnight.

I pushed him away and ran to the bed. The TV was on, and Times Square broadcasted their legendary Ball drop while I sat on all fours.

"Yeah, that's what I'm talking 'bout," he said, taking his boxers off and licking his lips. I looked at his erect dick that curved a bit but looked delicious as fuck. His body was rippled with muscles and tattoos.

"Lay down, let's 69," I said. He did as he was told, and before I could get his dick in my mouth, he was already tonguing my clit. "Ooooh, baby, you... sure... can... eat... some... pussy."

"When it taste as good as *you* do," he said, spreading my cheeks wide and tonguing my other hole. That shit felt so good I shivered. "I'll eat it all...night...long!"

I don't know if it was the Molly, the drink, or the few hits off the blunt I took, but I was feeling porn star freaky!

I licked his pole up and down, then rubbed it across my face. When I took him in my mouth, his whole body lifted off the bed. I smiled around his dick. There was no better feeling than *knowing* I was giving someone pleasure. His moans were valid signs that I was doing something right. His hard flesh felt like a hot, velvety volcano in my mouth. I mimicked his tongue motions so we could orally rock each other's world in sync. When he sucked my plump pussy lips, I sucked his smooth balls. He had that perfect-sized dick that would feel *great* inside my tight womb. It wasn't too big, and it wasn't too small.

I looked up at the TV. *Two minutes until midnight.* I grinded on his face. "Make me cum baby. Spread me open and suck the cream out of my pussy!" I spit on his dick and gobbled it whole. I felt his fingers entering me, and even with how wet I was, his minor intrusion was somewhat painful. The countdown began. *Ten, nine, eight...*

"Damn, you got a pretty pussy," he said and kissed my wetness.

Seven, six, five...

"Mmm, so sweet and...what the fuck?!" he yelled and pushed me off his face.

Four, three, two...

"Wh-Wh-What's wrong baby?"

"Your pussy. What the fuck is that in your pussy?!" he yelled and got off the bed.

"Happy New Year!" the TV announced as confetti rained down on Times Square.

My friends could be heard screaming Happy New Year as well while I sat on the bed in shock and in tears.

"Ay, look. No disrespect ma, but that don't look like no regular pussy," he said, scraping his tongue with his fingernails. The asshole was acting like I had a disease.

"Bruh, you bogus as fuck. Get out my room dude," I said.

"What I do? You're the one with an eggplant in your pussy, and it sure as hell ain't *mine.*"

"Huh? What the fuck are you talking about man? You're pissing me off."

He grabbed his phone and spread my legs. "Hey, don't you be-"

Click! Click! Click! I heard the clicks from his camera phone before I could get my legs closed.

"Look," he said, thrusting his smartphone in my face. My mouth dropped open in horror. *WTF?!* He saw the look on my face and nodded. "Yeah. You need to get that checked out."

On his screen was my vagina. It had a big, purple abscess inside the size of a baked potato. I asked him to delete the pictures.

"I will. Happy New Year ma. Sorry about my reaction, but..." he patted me on the shoulder, gathered the rest of his clothes, and left my room.

🎋 2 🎋

KING

I knew 2020 was gonna be a shitty year by how it started off. I thought it would be all good, but when the ball dropped, I was backing away from some alien pussy that I was *really* close to dipping into. Thank God I spotted the whatever the hell it was when I did. Shorty was bad, but that thing in her pussy had me scared to go down on *all* bitches after that.

"What's up, King? How was your New Year's?" one of my co-workers asked.

"Eh, it was nothing special." I lied and kept it moving.

I worked at a distribution warehouse for Fleet and Farm. Me and my boy Shawn were the only two brothas that worked in the whole place. There was a black chick who worked there that was cool, but she was a very manly lesbian who swore up and down she was a dude.

All the white women eyed me as I entered the huge plant. I had to walk two blocks just to get to my cardboard bailing station. During my couple-minute walk, I was always able to check out the honeys and see what they wore to work that day. Most of them wore leggings and tight T-shirts. When Shawn and

I first started back in August, they weren't rocking that shit, but as the time passed, the women's clothing got tighter and more revealing.

I was an avid admirer of the female body. A nice body always made me smile and brought joy to my day. I didn't need to talk to or fuck a woman to appreciate her beauty. At one point, I wanted to fuck every girl in the world, but as I got older, I was able to restrain myself a bit. Being able to look and do nothing more took great discipline for me, but it strengthened my character.

"Heyyyyy, King!"

"Hi King. How are you?"

"Ooh, I love your outfit today King," my regular "fans" commented as I walked to my workstation. It was a great ego booster to work with predominantly all women and have most of them flirt with me on a daily basis. Most of them weren't really my type, but I still appreciated all the love and comments I was given. Whoever said men didn't love compliments lied. I *thrived* off them.

I nodded and smiled as I reluctantly headed to put in ten hours of back-breaking work. I hated my job. It paid $15 an hour, but it was only Monday through Thursday. All my weekends were three-day events, and because I worked through a temp agency, I got paid every Friday. I thought it was bogus to have to come in for one day after New Year's, but the bag had to be secured, so I showed up feeling groggy as fuck and still buzzed.

I worked alone. My job was to put all the cardboard in a compactor and make sure the 1,000- pound bales were loaded on the back dock for pick-up and recycling. I also had to use an EPJ (Electronic Pallet Jack)- to pick up every single garbage can in the warehouse. I drove them to the dumpster, emptied each garbage can, and returned them back to where I got them from. They were heavy ass garbage cans full of dog food, rocks, cat litter, splintered pallets, and all kinds of other heavy shit. On average, each garbage weighed fifty pounds, so I definitely got my work-out on from doing a ten-hour shift. Every day I came home sore and tired, but my body was ripped with muscles from it. The ladies loved it, so I couldn't complain.

"How's it going King?" Josie asked me. Josie was second in command at the warehouse. She was married to a black man, so her swag and dialect were different than her colleagues. I liked her from day one. She had a fat ass and big titties that I wouldn't mind climbing on.

"Oh, what's up, Josie? I'm good. How are you?" I responded, already sweating from breaking down the refrigerator-sized boxes.

"Well, I survived the New Year, so I can't complain," she said and smiled.

Girl, you just don't know! I'll tear that ass up! I thought, while eyeing her delicious cleavage. "Yeah, I hear ya on that one."

"King, I know we aren't supposed to hire you on until next month, but a lot of people recently quit, so we'll be bringing on new temps and making the ones who've been here a while official employees. Are you still gonna join the team?"

"Uh, yeah. I get a raise, right?"

Josie laughed. "Yup. A dollar and fifty cent raise when you're hired on."

"Bet. I'm all in," I replied.

"Great! Come lunch time, I'll be gathering some of you to fill out paperwork in the main office. You'll also watch some orientation videos, stuff you already know obviously, but it's company policy to go through it with new hires. It'll take a couple of hours, and then you can finish off your workday."

"Alright. Thanks Josie."

"No, thank *you*, King," she said and walked away.

Everyone in the plant knew me and Shawn looked at women's butts all day, so, most of the women added sexy and sensual movements to their walks because they knew we were looking. Josie switched away making that wide ass bounce up and down like a basketball. *Mmmmm!*

"Bro, you talk to Josie?" Shawn broke me out of my trance as I took a break from baling cardboard. I turned around and saw a sea of white faces staring at us. He was the janitor, so he cleaned the bathrooms and offices. When he was done, he'd come help me out from time to time. We would sit by the cardboard compactor and comment on any woman working in our sights.

"About getting hired on?" I responded but was looking at a thick chick named Sabrina.

"Yeeeeeah boy," he said, sounding like Flavor Flav. "We finna get mo' money, mo' money, mo'," Shawn said, rubbing his palms together. "Dammmmmn, she know she strapped," he said, eyeing Sabrina with me.

"Hell yeah she is, dog," I replied. We both ogled the perfectly shaped bubble butt that jiggled relentlessly in Sabrina's gray leggings. She saw us watching and smiled as she walked over to us.

"Can I borrow this?" Sabrina asked, picking up a big cardboard box.

"You can borrow whatever you want, beautiful," I said.

"Thanks, King," she sang flirtatiously and walked away.

"Mmpf! She *throwing* that ass. Damn!" Shawn said, drooling.

"Mhm. She *shoooo'* is. She came over here just so we could see her walk away," I said.

"Damn, fam, you right. She know what she doing. Chun-un-ky booty!" Shawn sung his favorite saying. Whenever he saw a big butt, he'd sing "Chun-un-ky booty!"

I licked my lips and thought about my brief episode with Sabrina a few weeks back. We got frisky in the far end of the warehouse, behind a tall stack of crates.

"I've never been with a black guy, but ever since you guys started, it's all I've wanted to do," Sabrina breathed in my ear while rubbing my crotch.

I palmed her fat ass and was amazed by the softness of it. The girl's booty felt like the biscuit dough fresh out the can. "What have you been wanting to do to me baby?" I asked, looking into her gorgeous green eyes.

She dropped to her knees, unbuckled my belt, unzipped my jeans, and pulled out my semi-erect dick.

"Gotdamn! It is true," she said and took me into her mouth. She moaned before **I** did. In fact, she moaned louder and more than I did throughout the whole damn process. Sabrina was a true freak hoe!

"Mmm, you like that? Hmmm? You like my slutty little mouth on your big, black cock?" She spit on my piece and wiped her face with it. Spiderwebs of saliva and my pre-cum dripped everywhere.

I was loving that shit! Sloppy toppy was my favorite.

"Hell yeah. I love it. Suck that black dick, you nasty, little, white bitch!" I said and palmed her head as I fucked her face.

"Oh yes... talk... dirty... to... me!" She gurgled.

"Fuck yeah. I'm gonna cum in your slutty mouth, and I want you to go kiss your boyfriend afterward. Tongue him down reeeeal good!" I said and laughed.

Her redneck boyfriend was one of the whiteboys I couldn't stand at the plant. He didn't like me, and I didn't like him...but his bitch did though.

Just as Sabrina's gags got louder and the spit ran from the sides of her mouth, we heard a forklift coming. She got up immediately, leaving me on the verge of climax with a drippy penis.

"Shit, we gotta go," she said, putting her breasts back in her bra. The forklift was getting closer, but there was no way I could put my dick in my pants in its current state. I turned my back to her and told her to go. She ran like the wind as the forklift got closer. I covered my dick with my shirt and hunched over as I walked from behind the crates. An older lady I'd seen around the plant hopped off her forklift and waved at me.

"Howdy."

"Hey," I replied, trying to walk past her as discreetly as possible. The space between the forklift and the aisle was so narrow that my dick accidently brushed against her. She turned around and smiled. She was old and wrinkly but wasn't bad looking. I could tell her cougar ass was quite the looker back in the day.

"Well, well, well... what do we have here?" She grabbed my dick and stroked it, bringing it back to life. That old cougar lady took control of the

13

situation and went after what she wanted, I admired the go-getter in her
and gave her what she wanted.

I fucked her right there on her forklift. If Sabrina hadn't left me
hanging, I wouldn't have been so thirsty for a nut, but I needed release
badly, and Bambi's old ass was wit it. After that, she became a once-a-
week regular, and she hit my hand every time she got paid. It was a win-
win for the both of us-she got good dick, and I got some dead presidents.

"I'm gon' hit dat," I told Shawn as I vowed to tear Sabrina's
pussy to shreds if I ever got the chance. She got scared after
almost getting caught, so I wasn't able to catch her alone since
then.

"Pssh, you wish, fool." He challenged me. I had already
fucked over twenty women there, and many more were on my
"to-do-list."

I knew shit was sweet when a supervisor chopped at me on
my first day. Her name was Amber, and she was training me on
an Electronic Pallet Jack.

Out of the blue, she bust out and said, "Don't chu hate it when you
suck your boyfriend's dick, and you taste another tramp's pussy on it?" I
lost control of the EPJ and crashed into a pile of pallets. "Oh shit, are you
Ok, King?" Amber asked, rushing to my aid.

"Yeah, I'm good. Your um... comment caught me off guard," I said,
dizzy as I stood up.

"Oh, I'm sorry. I was just venting. I gave my man head on lunch
break and tasted pussy all over his Johnson."

I was stunned. This was my first day on the job. This bitch didn't
know me from Adam, yet she was telling me some pretty personal stuff.
She was either extremely comfortable with me, or she was with the shits.
I threw her some bait.

"Shiiiid, if you sucked my cock, it wouldn't taste like pussy. Just clean,
yummy, chocolate."

"Oh Gawwwwd, you're so hot. Come on, I know a little place we can
go," she said and grabbed my hand.

Five minutes later, we were locked in the first-aid room. I was leaning against a nurse station while the chubby brunette was on her knees gobbling me like I was her last meal.

"Mmmmm, King, you weren't... lying," she moaned and slurped on my dick. "Your cock is fucking delicious. I would blow you every day!" And she damn near did, unless I was getting nasty with another one of my co-workers, in what I dubbed "the freak room."

I didn't tell Shawn about my exploits because he would just hate on me and say I was lying. If only he knew... the same bitches he commented on and lusted after, I already had them in every way that I wanted. He was an old tender-dick ass nigga. He had an ol' lady, but he still lusted after every woman he saw. He talked like he would get at the honeys, but he was timid and scary as a muthafucka when it came to spittin' game. Not me though, I was a real G, spittin' real P, that had the women falling in love with me! A bad boy Dom doing my King thing.

"My nigga, please. You think I can't smash ol' girl? Whatever, witcho hating ass. Shiid, you better hurry up and fuck Jess before *I* slide on her."

"Nigga, you better stay away from my bitch. That's *my* pussy!" Shawn claimed.

I laughed at his ass. "Fool, how you gon' claim some pussy you ain't seen, touched, smelled or even tasted yet?" I asked.

"Don't worry 'bout that. You know she digging me, so fall back."

It was true. Jess was head over heels for my nigga. She was hands down the baddest female at the job. She looked like a young Demi Moore but with the body of Kim Kardashian. Jess was *super* strapped! I tried to shoot my shot, but she respectfully declined and told me she was feeling my boy instead. Me being the playa that I was, I pulled his coattails and put him in the car with her. But Shawn was shy. He talked that playboy shit, but he didn't follow through on it. He had a woman at home that he couldn't stand, but he loved her dirty draws at the same time.

"*You* the one who should be worried about tasting pussy. Let me see your tongue. It got any pus bumps on it yet? I think I see some lesions on your mouth."

"Man, stop playing," I said, carefully inspecting my mouth for abnormalities. "That shit ain't funny. That ho fucked me up. I'm having nightmares about that shit," I admitted. I was seeing huge, purple balls in my dreams. In one dream, I got jumped by six, seven-foot eggplants while Lil Wayne's *"6 Foot 7 Foot"* played on repeat. I shook the disturbing images from my head. "I ain't eating no more pussy fam. I don't care *how* bad the bitch is... ol' girl done scarred me."

"I feel you, dog. Damn, that's crazy. What do you think it was?"

"Man, I don't know. Her pussy was pretty, but when I opened that muhfucka up... Whatever the hell that was, bro, it was nasty as hell!"

"Ugh." Shawn shivered, "Alien pussy." We laughed and headed for the cafeteria since it was close to lunchtime. After we ate, a bunch of us went up front to the main offices where we had to watch videos and fill out paperwork on the computer. Midway through, one of the HR ladies dropped the bomb that we had to go up the street to the clinic to give a UA sample.

"What?" Me and Shawn exclaimed in unison.

"Yes, when you get hired on, you have to pass a drug screen," the woman informed us.

"We already took one of those through Express," Shawn said, referring to the oral swab we took before we started with our temp agency.

"Maybe so, but now that you will be official employees through the company, you have to take one with us."

Shawn and I looked at each other. We were both dirtier than a trailer park with no grass. Shit, I was still high from New Year's Eve, and they wanted me to drop?

"Oh, OK. So where do we go?" I asked. She gave us the information and told us to go once we were done with our onboarding.

"King, what the fuck we gon' do man? I'm high right now! How the fuck I'm supposed to pass a piss test?" Shawn whispered to me.

"Calm down, bro. I'll figure something out. Just stall for as long as you can. Take your time going through the paperwork," I informed him while I tried to figure out a way to save our jobs. Even though I was sore every day from work, the five hundred I got every week was helping me stay afloat. I had other side hustles, but at least my nine-to-five was guaranteed money that I could depend on being there fa sho fa sho. I did the math, and with my $1.50 raise, that would take care of my gas for the week. Shawn pitched in, but I did a lot of driving bussin' moves when I wasn't at work. I loved money. As a multi-faceted hustler, I had to get it.

"Bro, I got some clean piss if y'all want it," this white dude we worked with said. His name was Dustin, an emo dude with purple and blue hair. He bought weed from me from time to time, so I knew he was cool.

"Shit, hell yeah. I was just thinking about how I could get some," I admitted.

"I always keep me a bottle in the car. You never know when you might need it."

"Bet. I'll throw you some money or -"

"King, don't worry about it, man. It's all good. When we go, they can only test one of us at a time. I'll save enough for y'all, then pass it to you once I'm done."

"Hell yeah! That sounds like a solid plan to me." However, it was all a dirty scheme. I didn't know it until weeks later, but he used the good pee, then pissed in the bottle and gave it to us. We squirted it in the cup, thinking the piss was A-1. But nope, when the results came back that me and Shawn were dirty, they fired us. A hippie chick named Taylor told me he was jealous of us. That's why he sabotaged our U.A.

I need to talk to you in my office King," Josie said one Monday morning.

I went to her office where she broke the bad news to me. "Josie, I promise you, my piss was clean."

"Well, the results show that you and Shawn were the only ones who didn't pass the drug screen. I'm sorry, but we're gonna have to let you both go."

"That's bullshit Josie. Our piss was clean. You're telling me everyone else passed but us?"

She nodded her head.

"It's cuz we're black!" I shouted and stood up.

"King, my husband is black. And you know I let your black ass get away with murder around here. All the shit you done stirred up since you've been here," Josie said.

There had been a few cat fights over "the D," because a lot of them bitches were crazy, but I didn't intentionally start no shit.

Ya see, that bitch thought I was gonna go quietly after they done used our blood, sweat, and tears. Hell naw!

Shawn got his hand split open on the job and needed forty stitches. They took him to the hospital but didn't document his injury. He went right back to work twenty minutes later, knocking pallets of dog food out for that bread.

That's the thing about my people: we're going to get it rain, sleet, or snow, and ain't nothing short of death gonna keep us from chasing that moola. But shiiid, muthafuckas had me fucked up if they thought I was gonna get fired without compensation. Not the kid! She had another thing coming. I reached in my pocket and hit record on my phone.

Check...

"King, my hands are tied. I went to bat for you. No one can do the job you and Shawn do so well. But this is from the top. It's over my head, sweetheart," she said and stroked my face.

I looked up at her and saw the desire in her eyes. When I stood up, she attacked me. Her lips were a fiery passion of lust that feasted on me like I was a buffet.

"Mmmm, I've been waiting so long to kiss these big, juicy, lips," she moaned in my mouth.

She was a good kisser. My dick was rock hard and pressing up against her in no time. I palmed her ass and squeezed it over and over.

"There's no way I'm letting you out of here without getting some of this." She grabbed my dick through my jeans.

"Um, Josie, that's my dick you're grabbing."

"Mmmm, King, yes I know. And what a dick it is! No wonder you've had these bitches going coo-coo for Cocoa Puffs over your ass." She dropped to her knees and pulled it out.

"Josie, I don't think you should be doing that. You're my boss... plus, you're married."

"Oh puh-lease, King. What cha gon' do, report me for sexual harassment?" She laughed and slurped on my dick loudly. "My husband hasn't touched me in months. I need some sexual healing baby. Give me this dick... or I'll take it," she said and removed her shirt.

Checkmate!

Her perfect D-cup breasts stood firm when her bra came off. She pulled my head to her nipples, and I sucked and chewed on those puppies like a newborn baby would. It wasn't long before I had her bent over the desk, pulling her hair and slapping her ass while I pounded her wet pussy out.

"Ohhhh, King. You feel so good, baby. Soooooo good," Josie moaned. She held on to the corners of her desk while I clutched her fleshy hips and fucked her doggystyle.

*Every time I got in some new pussy for the first time, I **had** to show out! I might not ever hit it again, so I went all in.*

"You like that, don't you?" I asked between gritted teeth.

"Fu-uh-ck yeah. I-I-I dooooooo!"

My heavy balls slapped the backs of her thighs with each thrust I took. Whoever was outside her office had to have heard us. We were knocking shit on the floor, moaning, growling, howling, and screaming. I wanted to be heard.

"I bet your husband doesn't fuck you this good."

"Hell no he don't! No one has ever fucked me th-i-i-sssss good. Oh God, King, I'm gonna cum again. Awwwwww shiiiiiiiit," Josie exploded all over my dick.

I could feel her walls spasm as they clutched my pole and released a flood of juices that had my stomach wet. I pulled my drenched dick out of her pussy and walked around the desk to where her head was hanging. I grabbed a fistful of her hair, and she gladly said, "Ahhh," when I shoved my dick in her mouth.

She sucked her juices off greedily. Her suction cup of a mouth vacuumed my dick with great enthusiasm. She slurped my manhood loudly while looking me in the eyes. That was an extreme turn-on for me, and I wanted to pillage her pussy. I pulled her across the desk and stood her up. Our tongues wrestled passionately while I tweaked her nipples, making her moan in my mouth.

I bent her over the swivel chair and re-entered her hot wetness. We both moaned at the same time. A deep guttural moan of ecstasy that was equally felt. I could tell she hadn't had sex in a while. Not only was she tight, but the bitch was in heat!

I fucked her every which way. We went through multiple positions where I made her come several times.

"Awww shit, I'm 'bout... to... cum... Josie."

"Do it! Cum on my ass," she instructed.

I jackhammered her for a few more minutes before I erupted.

"Ohhhhh gawwwwwwd," I moaned as I splashed my seed all over her back and butt.

Sweat dripped off my face and landed on her body. We breathed heavily like we just ran a marathon. Once we caught our breath, Josie dropped to her knees.

"Allow me to clean this delicious dick up." She sucked our secretions off and licked me clean. "I'm really sorry King, but you're gonna have to leave the premise. Go clean out your locker."

I looked at her dumbfounded. "Are you serious?"

She nodded her head. "Hit me up on Facebook Messenger whenever you want to get together. I'm really sorry, King. I wish there was something I could do."

She didn't know it yet, but what she just did was more than enough. I exited her office with my head held high, a smile on my face, and my balls on empty.

3

QUEEN

I spent New Year's Day in the ER getting a Bartholin cyst removed from my vagina. After my embarrassing episode with ol' boy, I did my own investigation and saw that the throbbing inside of my hoo-ha was actually something serious. A big purple abscess the size of a softball was inside of me and causing a lot of discomfort.

They cut it open, drained it, stitched me up, and gave me some antibiotics. A week later, I was back in the hospital because my appendix had burst. The nurses were joking that I must like the 2020 version of the hospital, seeing that the appendectomy was my second surgery in a week. 2020 was definitely not starting off well for me, and since I had to take off work because of my health issues, money was funny as hell. I was running up credit card bills to cover things.

My bestie, Jenny, took care of me while I was healing. The pain once the drugs wore off was excruciating. I could barely stand up straight. I sat in my own funk, feeling depressed.

"Girl, this is just a minor setback for a major comeback," Jenny told me one day. I was laying on the couch, binge-watching Netflix shows while she kept me company.

"I hear you ma, but it sure as hell doesn't feel like a come-back the way I feel."

"That's cuz you're still recovering. You'll be a'ight, girl. Stop trippin'. The Queen I know holds her head up high and can make it through *anything!* You remember Jamal?"

"Shiiiiid, I wish I didn't," I replied.

If awards were handed out for "Piece of Shit of the Decade," Jamal would win by a landslide. I got involved with him after meeting at a music festival. He was a pretty boy, which should have been the first red flag, but I was mesmerized by how such a fine man was into me. Well, that nigga ended up being a nut job.

He put his hands on me a couple of times. I tried to forgive him and chalk it up to him being drunk, but common sense sunk in, and I realized that fool was an alcoholic. He drank a bottle of Remy Martin a day, and afterwards, he would get *really* mean. The only thing that kept me around for as long as I did was the sex. He was the best I ever had. He had a big dick and a mean fuck game that made me cum every time we did it. I could admit it, I was dick-whipped. Good sex would cloud any person's judgment.

After he fractured my ribs and threw me down two flights of stairs, I finally got a restraining order. I never understood why women would stay in abusive relationships until I was the victim in one myself. He would come home smelling like perfume with lipstick prints on his clothes and body. The first time I confronted him, he slapped me so hard I thought I was going back to the future. After that, it was an onslaught of abuse followed by "I'm sorry, baby." Flowers, trinkets, and other gifts that were sweet and seemed to soften the next blow came soon after, and like a dummy, I forgave him.

Enough was enough after the stairs incident. A couple of my male cousins found out and got involved. Jamal's pretty, yellow ass was beaten black and blue. They gave him a serious Pump-kinhead the size of an Escalade! They told him to leave me alone, but he refused to listen. He violated the restraining order, showed up at my job where I worked in home health care, and threatened to shoot my patients. An older guy named Earl tried to come to my rescue, but Jamal pushed him to the ground and beat him with his own walker. It was a disgusting sight. When the police showed up, Jamal was in demon mode, breaking dishes and tearing up the furniture. They had to tase him several times to get him under control.

I knew I would lose my job if they found out he was my ex, so I lied and said he was some deranged man that just showed up and went nuts! Even though I was raised not to "snitch," I had to testify at Jamal's trial if I wanted him to go away for a while. Otherwise, he'd get a slap on the wrist and come after me once he got out (which he promised to do). They gave him ten years in prison and another five years on extended supervision, Wisconsin's version for parole.

His confinement did little to settle my nerves. The months of physical and emotional abuse had rattled me to the point where I could barely function. I had to go see a psychiatrist for over a year before I felt some sense of normalcy again. There are still certain things that I see, or things men would do, that set off triggers for me and put me in a bad place mentally.

"Queen, you need a vacation when you get better girl. You done had two surgeries, missed a lot of work, and ain't had no dick in so long you probably forgot what it looks like."

"And *tastes* like," I added, and we both laughed.

"Girl, you so stupid. For real though, let's plan a trip. Just me and you. Where you wanna go?" Jenny asked me.

"Um, I haven't worked in weeks. You know I'm broke right?"

"Queen, don't even worry about it. It's on me. I'm finna get my taxes back any day now. Plus, I been putting in plenty OT, so I'm good. I wanna get away for a while myself."

I knew that was a true statement. Jenny was a single mother to a ten-year-old boy who was a handful.

"I can't let you pay for a trip Jenny."

"Shiiid, why not? You covered my gambling expenses in Vegas. I owe you ma."

That was also true. We spent a week in Vegas for my birthday. We came with five thousand dollars in a Crown Royal bag. That was our "gambling money," but we ran through that in four days. I withdrew another three thousand from my savings, which was all gone the night before we left.

"Jen, you know I'm not trippin' over that lil' money," I told her.

"I know you're not, but still, we both need a getaway, and it's on me. So let's look at destinations, and wherever you wanna go, we're outta here as soon as you're better."

I grabbed my iPad, and we looked up vacation packages. The doctor told me to chill for six-weeks, but with February approaching, I knew I'd want to go somewhere warm. Winters in Wisconsin were vicious! I always wanted to go somewhere overseas but opted for Hawaii. They had some good vacation packages for the main islands, so I picked Waikiki.

High-rise luxury Hotels lined the shore where beautiful, turquoise-colored water splashed on white sandy beaches. We stayed at a two-bedroom, two-bathroom beach resort that had a golf course, waterslide, cocktail bar, tennis courts, fire pits, and several outdoor grilling stations. We planned to do things I'd never done before like surfing, ziplining, Whale-watching, Volcano exploring, and attending a bomb ass Luau.

I always wanted to watch the Hula girls dance in their grass skirts and eat the delicious food they prepared. The one we went to was like a party and one of the best nights of my life!

"Dammmn, this shit is lit!" Jenny said as we entered the Luau.

Two beautiful Samoan women put colorful leis around our necks once they checked our tickets. To the Hawaiian people, greeting you with a lei is a symbol of love and friendship and a way of accepting you into their community. We felt very welcome in the festive atmosphere.

"There are complimentary drinks at the bar, and the roast starts in about an hour," a young woman told us.

We walked to the ocean where a huge stage overlooked the clear, blue water. Dozens of tables and chairs were set up for the guests to eat and watch the entertainment. I wanted to be early to get a good seat and soak up all the festivities. I picked seats close to the stage. We set our stuff down and headed for the all-you-can drink bar.

"Now *this* is what I'm talking about," I said, sipping a yummy Mai-tai.

"And these are free all night?" Jenny asked. We both looked at the two buffet tables full of all- you-can drink Mai-tai's in big, colorful bowls. It was self-serve, with plastic cups and drink scoopers in the bowls. Two bartenders stood at the end, topping off people's drinks with extra rum if they so desired. Me and Jenny desired extra rum in the two cups we each held *every* time.

"I'm gonna be drunk as a skunk before the night is over!" I shouted. We toured the Luau and took pictures. All kinds of fun games were going on - pineapple bowling, Hawaiian limbo, face painting, Hula hooping, and Ukulele lessons.

Tents were laid out for the buffet of Kalua pig, Lomi-lomi salmon, Poi, and many other Hawaiian dishes. At the imu ceremony, there was a history lesson followed by the uncovering of the pig ritual. We all crowded around the sandy pit where a three-hundred-pound pig cooked for hours in an underground oven, (better known as an imu).

Polynesian music, fire-wielding dancers, Sumo wrestlers, and belly dancing hula girls were our entertainment while we dined on the best pork I'd ever eaten. I was tipsy as hell, and to have real, authentic Hawaiian food was the icing on the cake. That shit was off the chain!

"For our next act, I'll need four volunteers to come to the stage. Our trained islanders will be teaching you how to hula live! Don't be shy now," the host goaded.

"Come on, Queen. Let's get up there and shake our asses girl," Jenny said.

"Bitch, we ain't at the club. This some whole *other* shit. And it's like a thousand people out here. I ain't trying to make a fool of myself," I retorted.

"Mhm, ain't nobody trying to hear that shit. Now, get cho ass up here," Jenny said, grabbing my hand and dragging me on stage. "Right here! Us two!" she shouted. The crowd cheered for us as we were the first two volunteers to come up stage.

"Come on, we need two more people to join these beautiful ladies up here. How about you sir, in the gray suit?" the host announced.

An older white man shook his head, but to no avail. Two hula girls went down to retrieve him from his seat. His wife clapped and cheered him on as they led him on stage.

"Anyone else care to join us? Come on, we only need one more person. They won't bite...unless you're into that," he said and laughed.

A handsome man that looked like Dwayne "The Rock" Johnson got on stage, and the women went wild. By now, all the alcohol had been drank, and everyone was intoxicated and feeling no pain. Hoots, hollers, and enthusiastic chants resonated in the air while the trained dancers stood behind each volunteer. I was lucky enough to get the big, hulky guy them bitches was screaming for as my instructor. Turns out, he was one of the dancers in the fire baton show.

The music came on, and he placed his hands on my hips. I could feel his hulking figure shadow me while the heat from his half-naked body made my temperature rise.

"It's all in the hips. Move them in figure-eight motions," he instructed, guiding me all the way through. First, he raised my left hip up, causing me to roll the weight from heel to toe on my left foot as my right foot was placed flat on the floor, heel touching the ground first.

I could feel his hard bulge throbbing against my butt and my nipples got hard. Even through my lace bra, they still jutted forward like two Hershey Kisses.

"That's it, gorgeous. Wind your hips just like that. Yessss, you've got it," he whispered in my ear. His breath was warm and smelled of Mai-Tai's and mints. His voice was deep and exotic, a sexy islander accent that made my cookie jar tingle.

I looked over at Jenny. She was damn near twerking on her instructor, who was trying to get her to slow down and properly do the dance. I laughed and shook my head. I was having fun and not the least bit shy about the hundreds of faces staring at me. The crowd's participation amped me up. Jenny was so lit she got everyone to stand up and cheer.

I was feeling better than I ever felt. Dancing on stage with the ocean behind me was my real-life backdrop as I pulled out my phone. I picked one of my favorite Snapchat filters and videoed all of us on the stage.

"Ayy! Ayy!" Jenny shouted in my ear while she stood behind me wiggling her tongue at the camera and throwing up the peace sign.

I captured everything from the pretty hula girls in grass skirts, to the off-beat white boy trying his hardest to catch a vibe, and of course me and my girl turning up. We were all full of alcohol, so the atmosphere was light and celebratory. The hula lesson was the final event of the Luau, and even though I didn't want it to end, I knew the night was still early. I looked at the moon and asked God to keep the night going for me and make it one to remember.

After the Luau, we exchanged information with a few cool people we met that were also visiting from various parts of the U.S. We went back to the resort, showered, changed, and hit the town. The nightlife in Hawaii was crackin' just like any other city, except their bars lined the shore where you can go out and see the tides roll in or put your feet in the ocean.

We bar hopped until we found a nice spot that had good music and a little bit more color in it. We drank and danced the night away. Facebook Live and Snapchat caught our wild shenanigans while we turned up and made new friends.

Two handsome brothers bought us drinks all night long. They were on vacation from Texas and had the country twang and gold teeth to prove it. I fully intended on hooking up with JJ, but when my hula instructor walked in, I gave my Texas groupie the cold shoulder.

"Hi, beautiful. How are you doing? Funny seeing you here," he said.

"Yeah, me and my girl been partying it up. When the bars close, we're throwing an after set at our spot," I told his fine ass.

"After set? What's that?"

I laughed lightly. "After party. You know, where you keep the party rolling for those not ready to go home yet?"

"Oh, OK. Sorry if I don't know some of your lingo." He smiled, and I looked at his pretty white teeth. He was over six-feet tall and very masculine. His bulging biceps were heavily tattooed and rippled with muscles. His skin was the color of butterscotch, and his clean-shaven face looked just as sweet.

"It's cool. So what's your name, handsome?"

"Hi, I'm Koa, and you are?"

"I'm Queen. Nice to meet you, Koa. Interesting name you have there," I said.

"Thank you, so is yours... Koa means brave and fearless."

"Ohhh, OK. That's pretty cool."

"You know what *ain't* cool? You ditching me for this muscle-bound muthafucka!" JJ snuck up on me and cut into our convo.

"Listen, young brother -"

"Yo, I ain't cho brother, nigga. Let's get that clear right now," JJ yelled.

Oh boy, here we go, I thought to myself and rolled my eyes. Why did men always have to cause a scene? "JJ, I'm sorry, I was just talking to him about -"

"Bitch, I ain't trying to hear your bogus ass excuses. You not feeling me? I'm J muthafuckin' J... from *Houston!*"

"Well, J muthafuckin' J... from *Houston*. If you call the lady out of her name again, I'm going to be forced to knock those pretty gold teeth out of your mouth," Koa said. That was the gasoline needed for JJ's fire.

"What the fuck you say to me, nigga? You think I'm scared of your big *Rock*-looking ass? Nigga, I done whooped mutha-fuckas bigger than you before! So,don't come at me like that. Shiiid, you got me fucked up! You and this bit -"

Before he could finish calling me another "B," my brave and fearless hero hauled off and punched ol' boy in his mouth. He hit him so hard, that he tipped over and fell flat on his back. His brother ran to his aid, and he also got knocked out. Bouncers rushed to the scene, and we scattered like roaches with the lights on.

"Dannnng, you knocked them mofos the *fuck* out," I said in amusement.

"Fuckers had it coming. I hate guys who disrespect women like that. Thinking they're all hardcore and tough," Koa said as we ran down an alley before cutting onto a main road. We blended right in with the other party-goers bar hopping and sight-seeing. He held my hand tightly as we soaked up the sounds around us.

DJ's playing dance music, drunk people laughing, and waves crashing to shore filled the warm night's air. I had on my little black dress, and the wind lightly lifted it from time to time.

"I know this is gonna sound corny, but I feel like I'm in a romance movie. My big, strong Hero comes to my rescue, we get away, and then walk on the beach until the sun comes up."

Koa laughed. "Is that what you want to do?" he asked and grabbed my hand.

I gave it a light squeeze and smiled. "Yeah, I do. I'd like that very much," I replied.

"The lady's wish, is my command," he said and scooped me up in his arms.

It caught me off guard, and I tried to pull my dress down

before all my business was on display. He laughed louder and ran with me in his arms to the beach, kicking his shoes off in the process. I carelessly kicked my stilettos in the air, and they landed somewhere behind us. I could hear the waves crashing to shore as we got closer to the ocean.

"God, this is beautiful," I said as he put me down. My feet molded into the sand as we gingerly walked down the beach.

"Yes, you sure are," he said and tucked a strand of hair behind my ear.

I blushed and looked at my feet. The butterflies in my stomach were confirmation that this was no movie and that it was actually happening to me. For 2020 to have started off so shitty for me, I was very thankful for the blessings I experienced. And if the world were to end tomorrow, I was going to make the most of what was in front of me *today*, no matter what it took.

"Last one in is a rotten egg!" I yelled as I ran for the ocean. Even holding my hem up to my ass, I was still faster than Koa. I was a track star in High School so I knew he wasn't going to hang with me.

"Woo-hoo!" I shouted as my thighs hit the cool ocean water.

"No fair, you didn't give me any warning," he griped, joining me in the water several seconds later. He'd stripped out of his button-down and jeans.

What I saw from the waist up made my mouth drop, and because I was wading in the ocean, I gurgled a mouthful of sea water. He swam to me when I began choking.

"Are you ok? Can you not swim?"

"Huh? Mpf, no. I'm...good. I'm ok," I sputtered, trying to swim away from him.

Koa wrapped an arm around my waist and pulled me to him. I struggled, trying to fight the inevitable, but my body wouldn't let me. My weak protests turned to moans of lust. My desire was making the ocean wetter.

My shoulder blades were pressed against his chest, and my

ass was pressed up against a weapon that grew larger and larger the more I grinded on it. Koa pulled my hair, yanking my head back until I was looking at the stars. I'm one of those bitches that *loves* her hair pulled. *Hell yeah, pull that shit daddy!* I said to myself. My head rested on his collarbone while my hair floated in the water. I reached behind me and massaged his dick through his boxer shorts. It was hard, long, and begging to be set free.

"Ohhh, Queen," Koa moaned in my ear when I figure-eight stroked him. The ocean was his slippery accomplice to the best hand job he'd ever gotten. I always had a sex on a beach fantasy, and he wasn't leaving until we made it come true.

I spun around in his arms and kissed his warm lips. They were soft as gummy bears and just as sweet. I knew I wasn't going to see that beautiful man again once I went back home, so I was going to make the most of it.

"Koa, I want to... feel you. *ALL* of you. On every inch of me. Make me feel alive again. Sex me on the beach and make my fantasy come true." I didn't wait for his response. I leaned forward and sucked on his bottom lip. When I wrapped my legs around his waist, I felt like the chick in King Kong's hand! I was never into body-building type dudes, but never having such a muscular man before made me want to see what he could do.

"I will sex you like the Queen that you are," he said and kissed me like he was never going to see me again. Our lips danced a passionate tango, and our tongues wrestled hungrily. "God, you are so beautiful," he looked into my eyes and said. He walked to shore with me clinging to him like a fanny-pack. "So, you've never done it on the beach?"

"Nope. Never," I said, stepping down on the sand.

"Well, rule number one is put something down to do it on, or else you'll have sand in places you don't want."

"Oh ok, so you're an expert on sex on the beach?" I asked, losing my courage to continue.

He could feel me pulling back and stepped forward. "Not like *that,* but I am from the island, so I have been intimate on the beach a time or two."

He was too cute. I couldn't help but laugh at his proper description of us doing the nasty. *Intimate on the beach?* Koa was a respectful gentleman. I was so used to bad boys that I couldn't fully appreciate how romantic and enjoyable he was trying to make the experience for me.

"Queen, we can just lay here and kiss and watch the sun rise. I'm not a panty chaser. We don't have to go all the way -"

"Alright, alright. Shut up before I change my mind. 'Go all the way?' Boy, you crazy. Now come here." I didn't care about the sand. I laid down on it in my thong and bra, and he lay next to me. I looked up at the full moon while he kissed my neck.

"Oooh, that's... my... spot... Koa," I moaned when he licked the area between my collarbone and throat. My pussy came to life in a roaring blaze of heat. My body reacted positively to his advancements. His big hands caressed my breasts, hips, and ass while his mouth explored my needy body. It needed to be touched, kissed, licked, grabbed, and fucked.

I rested on my elbows while my toes drew hearts and wrote words in the sand. Just as I began to zone out, my phone rang. I looked over at the screen, Jenny's face was flashing.

"I'm sorry, I gotta answer this...Hello? Hey, girl. What's up? I'm... I'm on the beach. Where you at? You ok?"

Jenny went on to tell me how she lost her phone in the bar and finally found it. Koa decided to be a naughty muthafucka and lick my belly button and kiss my stomach while I chatted with my best friend. I lifted my butt off the sand and let him pull my thongs off. The cool ocean breeze blew on my wet lips and I got a whiff of my sex. Koa did too because he wasted no time diving in.

"Huh? Um, I'm with a friend... yasssss, he's, mmm, he's cool," I moaned. "Huh? Yeah, I'm fine. I'll see you...back at the rooooooom." I hung up and threw my phone in the sand when Koa took my clit into his mouth and sucked on the hood.

His tongue painted swirls across my love button. The sensations and volts of electricity that went through my body were explosive.

"Mmmmm, you even *taste* like a Queen," Koa said between my legs. He sucked my puffy lips and slurped up everything I produced.

His enthusiasm turned me on even more. I clamped my legs down around his neck and flipped him onto his back. I spun around facing his feet and pulled his boxers down. Before I could get his hefty dick in my mouth, he was already tonguing my creamy center.

I held his dick in my hand and watched the tide roll to his feet. *Damn, I'm 69-ing on the muthafuckin' beach, in Hawaii!* I thought before I licked him up and down. His toes curled, and I smiled. I wanted to make that beautiful man feel like a King, so I pulled out all the stops and sucked him like I was a porn star.

"Oh my God! Kw-Kw-Queen," he stuttered. I licked and sucked his balls and watched his ass lift off the ground. "F-F-Fuck!"

I love to 69, but it's hard to concentrate on your designated task when your partner is delivering intense pleasure. I had to dial it down a bit because he was neglecting my cookie jar, but when I slapped his nose with my pussy, he spread my ass cheeks wide and darted his tongue in and out of me like a slippery snake.

"Oh, Koa. Koa. Koaaaaa!" I screamed when my orgasm washed over me like the ocean that splashed upon us. I spit on his dick and stroked it up and down aggressively. When I spun around, he was ready for me. I placed his fat manhood at my entrance and took a deep breath. I gasped when he first pierced me. It's nothing like a dick entering me for the first time. Getting used to the size and feel of it is the fun part. Feeling it make its way into my body is an adventure in itself. One that I enjoy immensely.

He pulled my bra straps down, and my perky 38C breasts

kissed the air. The cool breeze hardened my nipples even more, and he pinched them gently.

"Mmmmmmm," I moaned and hunched over him as I slid further down his pole. I threw my head back when he took my nipple into his mouth. My cries of pleasure floated to the moon while he feasted on my breasts and went deeper into my love cave.

"Ohhh, Queen. You...are...soooo...tiiiiiight," Koa sighed in ecstasy.

That compliment boosted my ego and helped lower my inhibitions. The alcohol had me feeling freaky too.

"Yeah? You like this tight, wet, pussy, don't chu, daddy?" I said as I rode him slowly. I wound my hips in circles so I could feel him stir up my insides. My pussy was the cake mix, and his spoon did the whippin'.

"H-H-Hell yeah I dooooo. Damn, baby, uhhhhh!" Koa threw his head back and howled at the moon.

When his eyes rolled to the back of his head, I put my palms flat on his chest and bucked him like a Bronco. He grabbed my butt cheeks and pulled me as far down onto him as possible. I could feel him in my stomach. A throbbing ache that hurt soooo good.

"Mmmm, it's been... soooo long... since I... had... good dick. Don't cum, daddy. I'm trying to enjoy this. Just... don't... ooh... cum yet," I moaned.

"Oh, you don't have to worry about that baby girl. I'm not going to cum until you've orgasmed at least *twice!*"

Now ***that*** *is what a woman wants to hear*, I thought to myself. An unselfish lover who was all about their partner's pleasure. My knees were digging further into the sand the more I ground on him. I rocked back and forth and gyrated side to side. I watched the pleasure on his face spread and radiate like the moonlight over the ocean.

I pounced on that dick like a pogo stick. His smooth balls rubbed back and forth against my ass, turning me on even more.

I could feel my first orgasm climbing to the surface. The buildup was intense, and my legs started to shake.

Koa sat up and sucked my nipples while I cried to the dark night sky. "Oh... my... uhhhhn!" The dam broke, and a flood of liquid heat poured out of me, drenching his dick and making the ride more slippery and loud.

"Yes, cum on that dick. Yeah! Ohhh, yeah! Get it Queen," he said between gritted teeth.

My body shook and convulsed while my orgasm spread from head to toe. "Ahhhhhh baby. Mmmmm, Koaaaaa!"

In one swift move, he flipped me on my back while still inside me and didn't break a stride. The seesaw moves that he pierced me with were so on point. His crown hit my G-spot every mid-stroke. Koa swiveled his hips when he was in me to the hilt, grinding on my clit in a rhythmic swirl that felt like fireworks in my pussy.

"Ohhh, Koa. Yes, just... like... that," I moaned. In my mind, I was thinking, *don't you stop muthafucka. Don't you dare stop fucking me this damn good!* I let my body do the talking. I wrapped my arms around his wide, muscular back and rested my ankles on his bubble butt. He gyrated his hips with every thrust, writing against my clit with his neatly trimmed manscaping.

We went at it for a solid twenty minutes of non-stopped thrust for thrust. I met him in the middle by lifting my ass off the sand when he was on his way back in. I clung to him. My hands never left his body. One minute, they were on his bald head, and the next, they'd be pushing his butt down harder. Mostly though, they roamed his back. My fingers traced his tattoos and the muscles underneath them in amazement. *Thank you, God,* I mouthed to the moon. He once again came through for me and answered my prayers.

Koa leaned down and kissed me passionately. His lips really were so soft that I literally thought I was sucking on Gummi Bears. *Who the **fuck** is this man?* I needed to flip the script, so I tested his ass.

"That's... all... you got? Huh? Mmm. I... thought you were going to *fuck* me on the beach? Pound this pussy, nigga. Beat this thang thang *up!*" I challenged him. I had my romantic back-drop, and I was covered in sand from head to toe, so at that point, I needed to go hard or go home.

"What?" he said, putting my ankles on his shoulders. His abs flexed every time he thrust into me. That shit was so hot. Koa held my calves and long stroked me with hard thrusts that drove my head further and further into the sand every time he went balls deep.

"Hm? That's... what... you... want?" He growled, plowing me with each word.

I didn't want to cum, but the way he was handling me made me erupt like a volcano.

"Ohh... oh... my... uhhhn," I mumbled as my entire soul exploded and shook like I couldn't motherfucking believe!

"Well, damn, someone was talking the talk and done came already." He boasted with a smile. He had me on that one. I kinda should've shut my mouth because ol' boy put it down! He didn't stop drilling me. I could see my juices painted across his stomach, and his sweat left salty drops across my breasts, neck, and face.

Koa kissed me and talked into my mouth while penetrating me so hard I couldn't breathe. All I could do was take short gasps of pleasure and ride the brink of unconsciousness and reality.

"Fuck you, huh?" Koa growled. "Is this... what... you... wanted? To be fucked. On. The beach. By... new...dick!" His dirty talk while fucking me senseless was on point, but he hadn't pulled my hair while fucking me yet, and when that happens - well, you know.

"Yeah, babygirl, that's it. Open up so daddy can go *deep!*" Koa said and rose up on his tiptoes and knuckles. There was a long pause while he planked me.

We both looked down at the tip of his dick being clutched by my glistening lips. I wish I could've taken a selfie of that shit. Just as I was admiring the moonlit ocean behind his smooth balls, he bungee jumped into what felt like my lungs.

I gasped for breath when his entire body pressed against mine. I thought a horse had just kicked me in the stomach and kept kicking me, over and over and over again.

"Mmmm shit. That's...it...daddy. Thaaaat's it," I moaned in his ear. I put him in a headlock and nibbled on his ear lobe and sucked all over his neck. His cologne mixed with our sex gave me a euphoric high that brought out the animal in me.

I pushed him off me and dove into his crotch. I sucked my juices off his hardness and moaned at my deliciousness. He leaned back on his elbows and spoke in tongues. I slurped up and down until nothing left of me was on him, and then I scurried away like a frightened mouse.

Koa breathed heavily as I circled him on all fours like I was a tiger. My eyes zeroed in on his sword that stood straight in the air, pointing to the moon. His eyes followed my sandy ass that swayed back and forth like the sexy feline I felt like at that very moment. I circled him several times before I stopped. I wiggled my butt and looked back at it. I wiggled my tongue like the waves a few feet from us.

Koa rose to his feet and slowly walked over to me. He stood there, shadowing me with his maleness. I licked my lips and wiggled my ass in anticipation as he knelt behind me. I could feel him trying to slide back in, and I threw my head back. The wet strands of my hair slapped my back, and I could feel the grainy sand slide down my ass crack.

SMACK! Koa slapped my butt cheek hard and made me yelp in pleasure. The further he entered me, the more I melted. *Then*, he grabbed a fistful of my hair and pulled my head back until he was all the way inside me.

"Ahhhhh!" I cried out.

He used my hair as a riding crop, pulling me back and forth by it, sending me on an orgasmic frenzy like no other. His balls slapped the back of my thighs with each thrust, and my elbows were getting raw from the friction in the sand.

SMACK! "Whose pussy is this?" **SMACK!** "Huh, Queen?" **SMACK!** "Whose is it?" Koa slapped my ass cheeks repeatedly while demanding to know whose it was.

"Ko-oh-uhhh, this... is... your... pussy... daddy. Ohhhh sh-i-i-it. Koaaaa!" Be careful what you ask for. I taunted him and figured he was just a romantic, love-making motherfucker (which was cool at times), but his fuck game was on beast mode. He flipped me around like a ragdoll, putting me in several positions as he claimed my body until the sun came up.

I came so much that my pussy went dry, and I had sand *everywhere*, but I didn't care. I dozed off on my prince charming's chest, listening to the birds chirp and the waves splash. The water rolling up to our knees woke us from a sound sleep.

"We should put some clothes on and get going. People will be coming to the beach to do their daily exercise soon," Koa commented.

"That's cool," I said and stood up. "I like to run myself. Maybe I'll get a couple of miles in before heading back to the room." I yawned, stretched, and looked around. Hawaii was such a beautiful island. I never wanted to leave.

"Oh, Ok. Well I have to be getting home. Gotta let my dog out to do his morning business." He told me to come to the Luau and see him once he was done later and I agreed. He gave me a hot, five-minute kiss that recharged me and had me dripping wet and yearning for another round.

I ran a few miles along the beach, then walked back to the resort with a sore pussy and a smile on my face. That man rocked my world! I had to have some *more* of that. A dude that sexy had to be taken. It'd be just my luck he'd be married with four kids or something. I pondered various scenarios Koa could be in and was on number six when I entered our bungalow.

"Girl, there you is! I was worried about you Queen. Are you alright?" Jenny bombarded me.

"Yeah, I'm ok girl. Is you ok?" I asked my BFF who was all worked up.

"Hell naw, girl. We gotta go. They shutting the airports down tomorrow, so if we don't leave today, we gonna be assed out."

"Huh? W-W-Wait a minute. Jenny, what are you talking about?

"Some virus from drinking Corona or something. Whatever it is, they shutting shit down... look." Jenny turned on the TV, and breaking news on every channel covered COVID-19.

4

KING

When Kobe Bryant died, it really put life into perspective for me. Death doesn't care how rich, poor, young, or old you are. When it was ready to come for you, the Grim Reaper will be at your door. It's not like I wasn't accustomed to the "here today, gone tomorrow" way of life; I grew up in the inner city. My friends and family died on a regular basis. Foes and frenemies did too. It's a sad way of life, but it was my reality.

I've been lied to, cheated on, abandoned, locked up, stabbed, shot, crossed, and seen some of the most horrific things no human should ever have to see, but it is what it is. I'm still here, and I let muthafuckas know *ain't no stopping me. I'm resilient as fuck!*

My walk, talk, drip, and sense of humor were how I told the world, *yeah, I'm in dis bitch. Even after all the bullshit, I'm still in this bitch! And I'm gonna live my life to the fullest.* My scars, ambition, and attitude are the proof of how much I could persevere and still keep striving.

I legally changed my last name to DOM on my 24th birthday. It was symbolic in many ways. After the only woman I ever truly loved died, it took me a couple of years to get my head on straight. She was born April 24th and always preached a *"do what you love 24-7"* mantra to me.

Because of her, I became a real-life DOM. Because of her, I learned about the Kingdom - spiritually, mentally, emotionally, and conceptually. They all have a dominion within my life.

After I changed my name, I went to the tattoo shop. My homie Poobie, owned one and was cold with the ink. We rolled 24 blunts and took 24 shots of Crown during the six-hour session. When I left *Poobie G'z Ink,* I had some nice ass body art that would remind me of my beliefs.

The Realm In Which God's Will Is Fulfilled was scrolled in a banner above the Mount Rushmore-resembling tattoo across my chest, except Washington, Jefferson, Lincoln, and Roosevelt weren't inked on my skin. Three faces that shaped and made me who I was were embedded on me. The fourth face was left blank for whoever deserved that spot. **KINGDOM** was tatted just below *Mount RealMore* (as I call it), across my abdomen.

IT'S FUNNY AS HELL WHEN PEOPLE FIND OUT MY NAME. Everyone swears it's a nickname until I show them my I.D. The looks on their faces be priceless. To be named King is one thing, but DOM as a last name? Most people think it's a play on Kingdom, the place a King resides, but it's deeper than that.

I moved a few hours north of my hometown to get more peace of mind and live a stress-free life. I had a few hustles going on, and up until losing my job, things were pretty gravy. I had all of 2020 lined up from my trips to the projects I was going to debut, however, sugar can turn into shit *real* quickly.

The muthafuckin' Coronavirus hit like a tidal wave of fuckery, and a shit-storm Tornado that tore every muthafucking thing up! Everything shut down. It was pandemonium in the stores. All the tissue and sanitizer sold out, you had to wear a mask everywhere you went, and plenty of companies were shutting down left and right. A couple of the chicks I talked to from my old job told me they were let go too. That was good news for the plan I had in store for their ass.

In the meantime, I invested in a few recreational drugs to flip and invested the profits into other money-making endeavors. My money had to make money. I wasn't a dummy. If I have X amount of dollars coming in and have to spend that on bills, what does that leave me? Nah. I was gonna double my money, double that money, then reinvest the profit while using the rest to take care of my financial obligations and treat myself every once in a while.

When I was working, it was full-time while the hustling and other shit was part-time, but the Corona had me slangin' full-time, and hearing the complaints and bullshit stories from my customers was a headache that I hated dealing with.

So many people be playing in their ass when I'm trying to handle my business in a timely manner. That shit was stressful as fuck, but I learned to accept my stress. I've hurt a lot of people, so it came with the territory. What separated me from the rest was my ability to channel my anger and disappointment into "other avenues." I took it out in a way that could benefit me financially, even though it took a toll on me physically at times.

WHAP! "One, sir. Thank you. May I please have another?" **WHAP!** "Two, sir. Thank youuuu! May I... please have another?" the four-hundred-pound woman moaned to me. She was a freaky, submissive chick that wanted to get beat and have a man cum on her face. Her husband was a square dude who didn't believe in nothing more than missionary, but he was married to a freak bitch that had to have it, and big mama paid what she weighed.

WHAP! "Three, sir. Thank you. May I please have another?" I whacked her ass with a leather paddle that would leave her sore for weeks. Her hubby wouldn't see her cheeks because he only liked her on her back anyways. I put a leather mask around her face that covered her entire head. The only opening was a small hole around the mouth.

A bondage mask took away her sight and smell, a double whammy in my sense-deprivation practice. When I took away a sub's senses, it sharpened the ones that remained and intensified their experience through compensating what I restricted them to.

I had that powerful, executive woman who worked for a billion-dollar corporation bent over and tied to my obedience bench. I had to get it specially made one for her since she broke my last one, but it was dope. It was like a black leather massage chair. The U-shaped headrest was just above the armrests. A small leather bench is what my subs laid their chests and stomachs on. I strapped their calves down to the leg stand and did whatever I wanted to do to them.

She wanted to let her freak flag fly, and I was the non-judgmental muthafucka who let her do her. I made two G'z an hour, and she got off without "technically" cheating on her husband. We never fucked. She just wanted her face used as a slut rag and to have her ass whipped. Sometimes I did go harder though.

I was still pissed about getting fired. *I bust my ass at work because I loved my job, and then they just throw me away like a used condom?* was my last thought before I blacked out. I whacked her butt cheeks over and over until I heard her scream the safe word.

"Country music! Country music!" she shouted and squirmed in her restraints.

I came to and looked around my playroom. Floggers, collars, gag balls, whips, chains, handcuffs, and sex toys of all kinds and variations stared back at me while I contemplated my next move.

I looked at the swollen marks on her buttocks and knew she'd be sitting funny for weeks. She whimpered inside the mask like a wounded puppy dog, but the streams of excitement that coated her pussy lips told me everything I needed to know. I dropped the leather paddle on the floor and walked around to the headrest.

"Can't hang, can you, slut rag?" She loved to be called

demeaning names that took away her power. "Country music, country music, are you kidding me?" I scolded her.

"I-I-I'm sorry, sir. I'm sorry for disappointing you. Please, punish me as you wish."

It was too late. The bitch fucked up my zone when she couldn't take the heat. Country music got her ass up out the kitchen *real* fast!

"Nah, we're good. Session's over for the day," I said and unbuckled the restraints.

She laid there and stretched her jiggly limbs out while I removed the leather mask. Her long dark hair was a jumble of matted curls that stuck to her sweaty head and flushed neck.

"Shit! Oops, please excuse my language Daddy. I-I'm sorry for using the safe word. I was losing count of the lashes. You were going so fast and so hard... I just... I don't know. I couldn't take it. I'm so sorry, sir."

I told her to get dressed and meet me upstairs. I didn't like having my sessions interrupted. Out of all my years in the lifestyle, I could count on one hand the subs who've tapped out. They signed up for the intense, the extreme, the volatile, so ceasing play was a serious action.

"King Dom, if it will please you, I will pay *double* the session amount. I'm really sorr -"

"Make it *triple* the amount, and I might be satisfied," I said with a smile.

She gave me the $5,000 for the original session in a Wells Fargo envelope. She sent me another eight grand through PayPal and I booked her for another session for the following month. It was by far the most I'd ever made for a Dom session. The money was great, but it took a lot out of me to switch into Dom mode because life was throwing so many curveballs my way.

I was out of a job and had bills to pay, so I had to do what I had to do. When I was 20, I was introduced to the BDSM lifestyle by this older chick I was seeing. She was a classy cougar who turned my young ass out and showed me all about the world of Kink. Two years under her care had my Dom game on point. When she died suddenly in a drunk driving accident, I went into a dark period of drugs and partying to fill the void of her absence.

A few family members staged an intervention and got me back on track. I went to counseling and rehab, where I was encouraged to express myself through whatever outlet made me feel better. That was writing songs and poetry. During my four-month stint, I learned a lot about myself and left a new man.

"King, you are a very handsome, smart, and funny individual," my counselor told me a week before my release. "You are only twenty-one. You have your whole life ahead of you. I know that your desire to succeed will keep you from failure. I believe in you King, but you have to believe in YOURSELF!" she told me.

"I hear you Karen. It's gonna be tough, but I know I have to get back on track and do something righteous with my life."

"I agree. You have more talent in your pinky than most people have in their whole bodies!"

I smiled at her. "Thank you, Karen. You're too kind."

"No, King, I mean it. I know you have trust issues with women. They either hurt you or leave you, but you have to accept that not everyone is going to like or love you all the time. And they sure as hell won't do it forever! All good things must come to an end unfortunately. Just prepare yourself for the aftermath. It's called softening the blow and knowing how to execute your plans even in the midst of chaos. Practice self-discipline and patience. It will benefit you someday." She held my hands in hers and gazed at me sincerely.

*"Life is short. Live everyday as if it's your last. Laugh, dance, scream at the top of your lungs from a mountain top. Tell the people you love that you love them, because you never know if it will be your last time seeing them. And remember this, King, as long as there is breath in your lungs, you can do whatever your heart wants, but you have to go get it. The world is yours for the taking! Make it your Kingdom and write your happy ending the way **you** see it. And don't stop chasing it until you are*

experiencing it. Dreams are real-life events once you make them come true."

The wisdom I learned from that woman molded me into a new man. A new King emerged from that experience. One I was thankful for happening. That was why she became the second face on *Mount RealMore.*

All I ever wanted to do was get paid. Fuck the fame, just give me those dead presidents that make the world go 'round. As a multi-faceted hustler, I had to learn that the game comes in highs and lows. At times, I might be all the way up, bussin' moves and making things happen. Then there are those dreadful setbacks and losses a muthafucka takes that knock a nigga *completely* off his square.

It wasn't always easy to get the money I once had, and it was even harder chasing the bag that I wanted so desperately to secure. That big payday that would have the fam straight and a muthafucka not worrying about bills anymore is *MY* "American Dream." Fuck living check to check. The have-nots *know* that feeling, especially when you come from the dirt and ain't got shit. It was ingrained in me to make something happen. Fuck slumming it all of my life. I was gonna chase that paper, by any means necessary.

I would've been one of those people that lived check to check if I didn't have my side hustles going on. The Coronavirus couldn't stop sex and drugs from selling. Those two would sell - rain, sleet, or snow!

"Man, you ain't got that last stuff you had the day before yesterday?" Jeff asked. He was a new custy referred to me by a friend of mine. He was an annoying guy, but he spent $200 every day, so I tolerated his ass.

"Man, I don't even know what I had then. I run through a lot of shit, bro. What, you didn't like what you got yesterday?" I asked him. We were in my Yukon Denali bussing the move.

"Nah, fam. That shit didn't even get me high," he whined. I

wanted to tell him, *Muthafucka, you do two hundred dollars' worth of drugs a day. It's only so high you can get!*

"Dog, I don't even know what to tell you. I always get it from the same dude, so while the product might switch up, the quality is gonna stay the same. Now here." I handed him an ounce of gas. "Take this. You gonna looooooove that."

"Word?" he said with bug-eyes as he smelled the bag. "Bet! Good lookin'G."

"No problem, man. Hit me up." I gave him a fist bump, and he got out my truck.

I pulled out the wad of money I made for the day and added his $200 to it. *"Respect the Game"* by Meek Mill came on, and I turned it up while I counted my bread. I had $1,640. Not bad for a day's work. I looked at those green pieces of paper and shook my head.

I've ruined a lot of relationships over the root of all evil, but I've also formed some long-lasting friendships over it too. It was a two-sided sword that cuts both ways – in the form of blessings, and in the form of curses. I wish I wasn't so driven by money and success, but it was hard *not* to be, when everyone told you you're not shit unless you have this, that, or the other.

No chick wants a broke, no-car-driving, no-job-having ass nigga, but a lot of dudes aren't where they want to be in life yet for whatever reason. I know I'm not, but it didn't stop me from striving to get there, and money is my main motivator. Once I get it, I'll know the type of success that I've achieved and what level I wanted to take it to next.

In the meantime, I kept doing me and I didn't give two fucks about what another muthafucka thought of me. I lived my life to the fullest every day I woke up. I'm good to others not because I expect the same from them, but because deep down, I'm a good dude that means well, even if I did fucked-up shit sometimes.

5

QUEEN

"You know that one guy that died?"

I looked at the old woman like, *WTF is you talking about?* She was the daughter of one of my clients. I was a traveling CNA that takes care of old folks. The pay is shitty for what I had to go through, but I love taking care of people, so the pros outweighed the cons for me.

"Um, excuse me?" I asked the wild-haired hillbilly. We were FaceTiming about her mother.

"That one ball guy. Uh, he plays baseball, or football, orrr basketball... I don't know. One of those damn balls, he plays. He died in that there plane crash -"

"Are you talking about Kobe Bryant?" I interrupted her.

"Yeah, Kobe, he..."

I tuned her out as she tried to explain how she had never heard of one of the most-famous athletes of all time until he died in a horrific helicopter crash. I mean, damn, there are people who I think were hiding under a rock all of their lives, but because of their way of living and location, they really didn't know any better. Naïve and green are the closet words I could use to describe them, but even that wasn't quite right. Thank God I got another call and was able to cut her off.

"Um, Mrs. Rollins, I have another call coming in. But yeah, everything is fine with your mother. Yes, yes. I'll do that. Ok Mrs. Rollins. Thank you. Have a nice day," I said and hung up.

"Damn girl, I am so glad you called when you did," I said, answering my other line.

"Girl, you got some toilet tissue?"

I looked at my phone after hearing my best friend's question. *What the fuck is her crazy ass on now?* "Is this nutjob day or something?" I asked her.

"For real Queen. These muthafuckas buying up all the tissue and baby wipes. This Corona shit got bitches fighting in Walmart for the last damn Sanitizer spray." Jenny laughed.

I giggled and shook my head. I could believe it. I saw some once-in-a-lifetime stuff when the Coronavirus hit. People lost jobs because the country had to shut down. Like, for real for real, the whole fucking ***world s***hut down, but Sanitizer spray?

"Jenny, are you high, girl?" I asked my best friend.

"Um, yeah, but what that got to do with anything? I'm serious girl. Ronnie shitty ass run through so much tissue. And wit' us only being able to get fast-food -"

"TMI mama. T-M-I." I cut her off to spare her number-two spiels I was about to hear. "I have a box in the garage. Just come by and get it. I'll be home by 7:30."

"Oooh, thanks, Queen. I love you."

"Love you too," I told her. After I hung up with my BFF, I looked over at Mrs. Sterling and thought about that word "**Love**." Here was this ninety-something year old woman being taken care of by a complete stranger (me), because her kids would rather pay someone else to take care of the woman that birthed them. *Did they not love her enough to do it themselves?* She wiped their asses when they were babies, but now, they were too good to wipe hers and change *her* diapers? *Hmpf.* Funny how life forces us to look at things from different perspectives when certain situations occur.

But what is love then? Is it caring for an elderly parent? Is it disowning your child after a dumb decision they made? Is "tough love" even a real thing? And what are the components and criteria that make up the word "love?" All of these questions went through my inquisitive mind, but the one I wanted answered the most was why **I** couldn't feel that thing called love? What all the happy couples bragged about is what I was missing. I mean, I had it before. Numerous times actually, and if felt great when I was in it. However, I also lost it numerous times too, and I swear it didn't feel good when I was *out* of love because another playboy played with my emotions and broke my heart.

I was in between relationships at the moment, and I was a little bit lonely, so my best friend's *"I love you"* turned me into a sappy sack of emotions in Mrs. Sterling's bedroom. She snored peacefully as I watched her massive frame rise and fall beneath the colorful quilt. I sat in the recliner next to her bed and picked up the remote.

There was nothing on TV besides updates about COVID-19, and I was soooo over all that madness. I looked at the nightstand that contained a marble chessboard and elegantly handcrafted ivory pieces. It was my traveling game of choice that I brought with me everywhere. It was how I cleared my head and formed new thought patterns. That might sound weird, but it was kind of instilled in me to think on another level.

My mother named me Queen because she was determined to raise a daughter that was treated like something, and what better way than to *literally* name her child something that everyone would be forced to call her? Well, because that's my name. For the most part, it makes me feel good when people say my name, especially watching it come from a sexy ass man, but it has its downfalls too. A lot of people expected me to be on some kind of high and mighty pedestal because of my royal name, but I'm far from the stuck-up type. My mother on the other hand? She was just a different kind of breed.

Her baby daddy (my father), was a one-night fling with a guy who fooled her into thinking he was "different than the rest." On her quest for love, every guy she got with after my father was the same way. So many dudes had played her, she grew to be a bitter, man-hating woman.

Mom had a "trust no man" motto that she tried to drill into me. Notice I said "tried." I was smart enough to know that if she didn't practice what she preached, why should I? While she tried her hardest to steer me away from the opposite sex, my boy-crazy ass desired that forbidden fruit even more!

Posters of my favorite actors and boy groups made me yearn for hot guys that were *way* out of my league. Again, even at a young age, I was always a realist. I knew Tyrese's fine ass wouldn't be getting on my school bus and serenading me, but it was nice to *think* that could happen to me. It's the same reason why people play the lottery. It's a fact that someone wins. But for the millions of people with losing tickets, it was all just a dream. A fantasy. A hope that maybe *their* luck would change for the better.

Living through my celebrity crushes was my escape from the real world. None of the boys at school liked me because I was an average-looking girl with a nose that got talked about a lot. It made me self-conscious, but it also gave me the tough skin to weather the bullies, rejection, and failure. Throughout my life, I rode all three (sometimes all at once), like a roller-coaster ride. From experience, that shit was *not* fun. Luckily for me though, I had a few non-judgmental friends that kept my life from being totally mundane.

Jenny was my ace boon coon, my ride or die bitch that I had known since kindergarten. Both of our mothers waitressed at the same diner, so Jenny and I spent many nights at the same babysitter's house.

My girl, Sarah, stayed across the street. She was the only mulatto girl on our block. Sarah didn't know who her father was, because her mom got knocked up by one of her johns when she used to turn tricks. Her Daddy issues ran deep, but she was a very good person.

Nikki was the wild-child, hippie girl of the click. Her mom was a big civil-rights activist in the sixties, so Nikki was brought up to be a free-thinking radical that had no love for "the man" and had weed for a blood type. I bet she could out-smoke Snoop Dogg if she wanted to.

To say that we were BFF's would be an understatement. We all had been to hell and back, but we were still a down ass team after all these years. All of us were pretty much single. Tired of the fuck shit the fuck boys put us through, we vowed to stay single until God blessed us with some loyal Kings worthy of our love.

Even though not having someone to cuddle up next to at night got depressing at times, I was loving getting to know and find *myself* again. After being dependent on a man to make me feel whole for so long, I lost my identity. I took our clique's challenge to the heart and really worked on being the Queen I could be proud of.

Still, my one magical night in Hawaii had me conflicted. If love were my next destination, I'd want it to be in the arms of Koa. I couldn't stop thinking about him. He was big, strong, romantic, sweet, and the man's sex game was bananas! I was emotionally sick that I didn't get at least *one* message from him. I hadn't spoken to him since my last night in Waikiki, so I figured I was just another one-night stand in his list of many.

I looked at the Chessboard carefully. Mrs. Sterling and I would spend an hour or so a day playing each other. Just when I'd be getting into my groove, she'd tap out and want to go to sleep on me. I couldn't fault her though. At that age, who wouldn't want to just eat, kick it for a minute, then go to sleep?

Love.

Was there a move I could make to attain it? A Queen without a King was just an independent ruler on the throne, but alone, nonetheless. I wasn't trying to grow old and alone like Mrs. Sterling. I looked at her, then over at the chessboard. *What's my next move?*

🐾 6 🐾

KING

It took a while for me to accept who I was and why I did what I did. Most niggas are in denial about their dog ass ways. Me? I embrace mine fully. Fuck it. It is what it is. Yeah, I'm a dirty ass nigga. So what? At least I could admit it. My past experiences molded me into who I am.

They say a dog is something that humps everything it sees, and can sniff an ass coming from miles away. Wellllll...

"You dog ass nigga, get the fuck out my house!" Treecy yelled to me.

Was she wrong for calling me a dog ass nigga? No, not really. I mean, I kinda sort of am. I mean, I did fuck her best friend. Was she wrong for saying her house? Hell yeah! Especially since all of the furniture, appliances, and tech gadgets in that muthafuckin' house was purchased by me. Plus, the rent was paid by my cold, hard cash, so she had it twisted if she thought the crib was all hers. I'd have her sitting on hard wood floors in that muthafucka if she thought she was gonna send me packing with my tail wagging between my legs. Only thing I'd leave behind is what she came with, and that was dirty dishes and some ibuprofen for her headache-giving, migraine-having, nuttier-than-a Pecan-tree-acting self!

I had several cribs, so I really didn't give a fuck, but I put a lot of money into me and Treecy's crib because it was a big ass, three-bedroom townhouse in an upper-class area. On some real shit though, I was bogus.

Shaniqua was her homegirl. They'd been cool for a minute, and what can I say? I knocked her back, and ma walked in on us and went hard on me.

"Um, I'll leave, but all this shit that I bought is coming with me. So I suggest you get a sleeping bag or air mattress, cuz it's not comfortable sleeping on the floor at night," I told her.

She looked from me to Shaniqua and growled as she kicked off a cat fight.

"Punk ass hoe! I knew you always wanted what I have!" Treecy yelled as she held Shaniqua's ponytail in a vice-like grip.

Shaniqua's head was down, but she still saw Treecy's exposed stomach. She took that opportunity to punch her in the gut.

"Oompf!" Treecy exhaled as she doubled over and fell on my lap. I was still naked, so my pussy-drenched dick slid across Treecy's face.

"Yeah, bitch. How my pussy taste?" Shaniqua taunted as she hopped off the leather couch. She got behind Treecy and grabbed her hair. When she began slamming my girl's head on the floor, I had to intervene.

"Yo, yo, hold up, ma. You done gave her all the smoke she wants. Now get off her."

"You better check your bitch, King. We cool ma, but yeah, you're right, I did want it. And? So what? I just got it too! Now what?" Shaniqua yelled at my woman, who was sprawled out on the living room floor. Living was probably the last thing Treecy wanted to do at that moment.

Shaniqua was a ghetto ass, nasty, freaky chick, and I have a weakness for those kind of sexy ass thots. The woman that stood over me yelling obscenities was a mellow, professional woman that was more "square." I liked her and all, but she couldn't be thotty if they taught a class on it, but that wasn't her fault. She was just being herself, and I loved who she was. She was a good ass woman. *So why the fuck did I do her bogus like that?* I thought to myself. I looked across the room at the mirror on the wall. *Cuz I do fuck shit when I don't give a fuck sometimes.*

Shiiid, I'm a roughneck nigga. No doubt about it. I'm a bad boy, but I have good intentions. Even when I'm bogus, I shrug it off and try to make amends. Even when that becomes a repetitive cycle, I just keep going hard. That's what some of the honeys dig. A nigga who can beat it up street style, drip G-style, and genuinely make them smile. That was the ingredients to getting a good woman. I knew how to attract them, but keeping them, on the other hand was a different story. Still, I wasn't sweating having no woman. they came a dime a dozen.

That episode with Treecy was a minute ago. There have been similar and wilder situations that popped off since then. I just rode the rollercoaster of events that life threw my way and kept it moving. My sex life was an interesting map of exploits that I tried to enjoy when I could, but for the most part, it was Money Over Bitches, and I tried to focus on getting my cash.

It's so much pressure on a man to provide for everybody and they mama, that he does whatever he has to do to show that he is the King worthy of *thee* crown. My mother made sure I would have to live up to such a responsibility. She named me after what everyone these days aspires to be - even me. Was I there yet? *Eh.* It was give or take some days. There were times when I was on top of the world, flying high, ballin' out of control, and living it up. Then there were the times when I had to start all over, re-group, go back to the lab, pull myself together, and find my way in life again. It was a pain in the ass and extremely frustrating at times, but real soldiers persevered where I come from. There's no quitter in my blood, so I just kept on keeping on and stayed optimistic.

It was tax time, which meant it was go-hard season on every level because everybody had some money. I was on "break a bitch" mode, so I was going extra hard on the internet. From dating sites to social media sites, I was talking to as many women as possible. There was a chick that lived forty-five minutes north of me that I was meeting for a first date.

She was in her late thirties and thick with long, black hair. We met at her favorite spot, Todd's. It was a small nightclub slash bar that played dance music and had cheap, strong drinks. She wore a red dress and heels. Her perfectly rounded face was pretty and welcoming. I greeted her with a hug and smile, but when she smiled back, my face froze. *Damn!*

How someone was so pretty but didn't have *any* teeth in their mouth was beyond me. Her grill looked like a Jack-O'-Lantern. I tried to think of all the pictures she had sent me. She smiled in a few of them but never enough to show her teeth.

"Nice to finally meet you, King," she said and grabbed my medallion. "Oooh, nice bling. Can I wear it?"

Strike one was the bitch having a raggedy ass mouth. Strike two was grabbing my jewelry and asking me to wear it. "Umm, so this your hangout, huh?" I asked and took a step back.

"Yeah, this my spot. You never been here before?"

"Nope," I told her, but I was gonna start going more often. It was way more women than men in that bitch. There were bad chicks of all ethnicities walking through that muthafucka too. The front part of Todd's was the bar area. There were dart boards, three pool tables, and a few poker machines surrounding the bar. Once I walked down the hallway, I entered the Night-club area. A big dance floor with mirrors on the wall is where the party was at. There was a DJ booth in the corner, a stage, tables, and stools along the wall. A mini-bar sat near the entrance.

"I'm a hoe. I know I'm a hoe,

But don't you call me that little nigga that shit come wit' da smoke..."

I heard the Yo Gotti song banging from the club area. I took a peek and saw plenty of women (mostly with their boyfriends), getting it in on the dance floor. I had to find a way to break it to ol' girl that I wasn't gonna be in her presence too long.

"Hey, babygirl, what kind of drink do you want me to get you?" I asked her as I eyed the multiple women fucking me with their eyes at the bar.

"Well, I love tequila, so I'll take a double shot of Patrón," she replied.

Of course you would. I strode to the bar, dripping sauce and smiling. I wore turquoise Balmain jeans and a matching shirt that had *King* scribed across the chest. A rainbow of colors was splashed all over the shirt like someone flicked a still wet paint brush at me. I wore matching Nike Air Max 90's and a turquoise Milwaukee Bucks fitted hat. My ears, neck, wrist, and fingers were all blinging hard under the blacklights. I eyed the hungry looks boring holes in me.

"Hi, handsome. How are you?" A pretty blonde asked me.

"Shiiid, I'm pretty good now," I said and flashed my best smile.

"Hi, I'm Shelly." She introduced herself and shook my hand.

"I'm King," I replied and pointed to my shirt.

"Oooh, nice name, your majesty," she said with a smile.

I laughed and checked her out. Not bad, eight in the face and a seven on the body tip, but I was checking out all the other potential in the bar. I'm one of those dudes that wears sunglasses at night. Bright lights fuck with the astigmatism in my eyes, so I pretty much keep them on to keep from having severe migraines. I especially had to wear them in the clubs where the lights were bright and flashed constantly. That also helped me look at the women without them knowing too.

From where I was leaning against the bar, I could check out everyone in my vicinity. Behind Shelly was a drunk couple making out heavily. A few stools down were a bunch of people shaking for shots. Across from me was a homely looking native chick staring at me and counting a stack of cash. That definitely caught my eye, and I stopped surveying the bar to focus on her.

She had a big nose that was probably broken two or three times. Her long, jet-black hair fell to her ass. She had some nice titties covered in tattoos that spilled out of a low-cut shirt. She even had a couple of face tats. I could tell she had some hood in her. She was surrounded by more Native-Americans who were all sipping Coronas.

A bunch of rowdy white boys were playing pool and drinking Jack Daniels. All the video poker machines were full, and two sexy bartenders were running back and forth serving drinks.

"Excuse me, what kind of Crown ya got?" I asked.

"We've got apple, vanilla, and regular," the Christina Aguilera-looking bartender said.

"Can I get two double vanilla's on the rocks?"

"Sure," she said and went to make my drinks.

"I'll pay for those if you promise to dance with me later," Shelly said.

"Bet," I replied and sipped from both glasses when they were given to me. I looked at my date, but she was occupied on her phone, so I took that opportunity to walk to the back where the dance floor was located.

All eyes were definitely on me as I stepped on the floor. I got a few smiles and waves, which I returned. The women used my presence as an excuse to get wilder. Their dance moves became more sexual and aggressive. I stepped right in the middle of the floor, held my drinks over my head, and swayed to the music. When the "Cha Cha Slide" came on, I sat at an empty table.

"Everybody, clap your hands..."

I watched in amusement as the drunk and uncoordinated people tried to follow the steps. I saw my date step in and look around before she spotted me and headed over.

"Hey, you. Did you forget about me?"

"Ummm -"

"Well, you obviously forgot what kind of drink I asked for, cuz that don't look like Patrón to me!" she said with a hand on her hip. The audacity of the bitch. "What is that?" she asked, pointing at my half-empty glass.

"Vanilla Crown," I replied but was looking at the dance floor.

"Eew, that's disgusting."

"Sorry you feel that way babygirl, but a King must have his crown."

"And what about me?"

I shrugged and spotted the Native chick entering the club area. She looked around the room and when she spotted me, we locked eyes. She smiled, and I was pleased to see she had *all* of her teeth. She sauntered over to me.

"This yo' girl, Daddy?" she asked. Up close, she was actually kind of sexy. She had some gorgeous, hazel eyes and full, glossy lips that I bet could suck a hell of a dick. Her perfume ignited my senses, and I sat up straight.

"Nah, I just met her."

My date smacked her lips. "What the -"

"Bitch, I suggest you lose the attitude and get lost. Me and this fiiine brotha has business to discuss," the native woman said.

Ol' girl knew a gangsta chick when she saw one and didn't want no smoke with her. She kicked rocks real fast.

"Mind if I sit down?"

"Not at all. Go ahead," I said, pulling out a chair.

"Thank you. I'm Yellow Thunder, but most people just call me YT."

"Hey, YT. I'm King." We shook hands and I looked at her delicious cleavage.

Yellow Thunder was covered in tats. She had both sleeves and her whole neck inked up. I was pretty sure the rest of her body was probably tatted the fuck up too. There was a yellow lightning bolt on her temple and a colorful feather over her right eyebrow. Her nose was fucked up, but I found it oddly sexy. The music was loud, so we leaned over the table closer to each other.

"King, huh? Well, hey there daddy. I know you're not from around here."

"Nah, I live an hour away. I just came here to meet ol' girl for the first time."

She laughed. "Who? Raggedy mouth?"

I laughed too. "Yeah."

"That bum ass bitch ain't on shit. She be meeting motherfuckers online and luring them here. Get 'em drunk so she can get the D is her plan."

"Shiiiid, that hoe ain't getting *this* dick," I replied and finished off one of my drinks.

"Yeah, I could look at you and tell you have higher standards than her meth-smoking ass."

"Whaaaat? How do you know she smokes meth?"

"Cuz I sell it to her, bruh. And where the hell do you think all her teeth went?" YT laughed.

"Damn." I shook my head and contemplated my next move. A hustler chick in a foreign city was at my table. "So, you be pushing up, huh?"

"Yeah, any coke, meth, or molly that gets sold in a three-county perimeter of this muhfucka comes from me and my team. I'm from the Rez, but I be moving and grooving all around these parts. You fuck around, King?"

"Nah, I just be working and shit." I lied. "I smoke a little green and pop X sometimes, but nothing too extreme."

"Mhm, that's why you got on like $20,000 worth of jewelry, huh? Nigga, I know my ice, I know that shit ain't fake."

"Most of my jewels were gifts," I said, which was true.

"Hmpf," she grunted. I knew she wasn't buying it, but I didn't know the bitch, so I wasn't about to put her all up in my business.

"If you say so, *King*. It's all good, baby. I don't give a fuck how you get it. Your drip speaks for itself, so I know you're not a bum ass nigga."

"Nah, I'm too ambitious to be on bum shit."

We chopped it up for like half an hour. She got a business text and had to make a run. She promised to be back before midnight, and I told her I'd stick around. Before she left, she put two Franklins on the bar and told the bartender to pour me strong drinks of my choice.

I was tipsy off Crown and dancing with every chick on the dancefloor. When the guys who weren't dancing with their women saw me on the floor, they hurried up and got their no-rhythm asses out there or tried pulling their girls off the floor.

I never understood jealous ass men. Like, you brought your woman to the club. She clearly wants to dance and shake her ass, so let her. If I knew a chick came with someone, I would be respectful (nine times out of ten), and keep things "PG."

I spent most of my time being sandwiched between two women - One grinding on my dick and another rubbing her titties on my back and grabbing my ass – while I captured our dancefloor antics on my Snapchat story.

Once a song came on that I wasn't feeling, I used that opportunity to exit the floor so I could cool off. I used the bathroom and grabbed some more drinks. On the way back to my table, a skinny, ugly, flat-booty white girl jumped in front of me.

"Why you gotta be filming everyone?"

"Excuse me?" I asked, wrinkling up my nose like I walked in an outhouse or something.

"You keep recording all of us. Put your damn phone away. No one said you can record us."

"Umm, first of all, I sure as hell ain't recording *YOU*. Now, get out of my way please."

"No, I will not move until you show me all of the footage you've recorded."

I laughed at her and pushed past her. That bitch was trippin' if she thought I wanted her ugly ass in my clips. I didn't even remembered seeing her until she approached me.

"Hey, I'm talking to you, buster. Don't chu walk away from me."

"Bitch, you better get the fuck outta my face. I'm not recording you, but I'm about to start recording you bothering me," I said and pulled out my phone as I took a seat at my table. She quickly scurried away.

A few minutes later, some redhead white dude walked up to me. "Let me talk to you for a second bro."

I slammed my drinks on the table and stood up. "What up, **bro**?"

"You called my girl a bitch, bro?" he asked. The ugly chick sauntered up to his side with a Truly in her hand and a big smile on her face. She was cheesing like I was about to get a first-class beatdown or something.

"That's your girl?" I pointed to the rude bitch that didn't know her place. Just then, I saw YT come back into the club.

"Yeah man, that's my girl. She said you disrespected her." The Opie Taylor-looking dude said.

"Listen man, you need to check your girl. I'm minding **MY** own business, and she comes up to me talking about recording her. No offense, but I haven't, and wouldn't, record *her*. So you can miss me with all that other shit."

"Miss you? What —"

"Is everything cool, King?" YT asked when she walked up to us.

"Nah, everything ain't cool. These two have a problem with me for whatever reason."

"Well, if you stop recording us, we wouldn't have a problem!" the chick screamed.

The whiteboy put his arm around my shoulder. "Come outside and talk to me bro. ***Oompf!***"

I punched him in his stomach with a swift right uppercut.

YT was quick and 'bout that life. She punched ol' girl in the mouth so hard that a tooth and blood flew from her mouth. She fell like a ton of bricks. The white boy tried to swing off, but I side-stepped it and clocked him in the chin. Just as bouncers rushed the scene, YT grabbed my hand and led me to the stage. There was an exit door that led to the patio behind the stage. We ran outside in the cool night air and into the alley.

"Damn. Drunk ass white people always think they tough." YT breathed heavily as we caught our breath and walked.

"I know, right? Muhfuckas can't even have fun without a muthafucka starting shit. And they say niggaz is bad. Hmpf!"

"Well, they wanted some smoke, and they got what they were asking for," she said. YT walked me to her Lexus truck. We got in, lit a blunt, and chopped it up while listening to music. She was cool as a fan. I learned that she was a Navajo that took her per cap money and invested in the dope game. She had two brothers and two sisters who sold for her and a teenage daughter that was wild.

"I can't believe you have a teenager," I told her, after she revealed to me something her daughter did.

"Believe it daddy. She gon' be seventeen on the 31st. Bitch think she grown too!" YT laughed.

"Shiiid, you probably did too. I know I was grown at a much-younger age," I said but didn't reveal just how young I was when I was forced to grow up.

"Yeah, you're right about that. That's how I ended up having her when I was 16," she told me. "But fuck all that, King. You're only as old as you feel, and my heart will forever be 21!"

"Ok then, get it ma." I encouraged her as I hit the blunt. Without warning, Yellow Thunder reached over the console and unbuttoned my jeans.

"Thanks for the green light. I'll get it alright," she said and reached inside my boxer shorts.

I tensed up because she took me by surprise, but once her smooth hands caressed my dick, it was over!

"Mmmm, King. Is your last name...Kong?" she looked into my eyes and said right before she took my dick into her mouth.

"Ohhh shit," I moaned. I might have been limp when she first grabbed it, but her velvety mouth got me to full mass right away. "Damn, YT, what chu onnnnn?"

She pulled my dick out her mouth, slapped herself across the face with it, then spit on it. "You see what the fuck I'm on. Now shut up and enjoy this sloppy toppy." With that, she inserted me back into her wet mouth. She licked, sucked, nibbled, slurped, kissed and erotically worshipped my manhood while I reclined in her passenger seat.

Everyone has their preference to where they like to cum. I prefer to cum in a woman's mouth. It feels better and is "nastier" for my kinky tastes. I don't typically announce when I'm about to cum because I want to see the woman's response when I do. Will she spit, or will she swallow? That is the question.

"Mmmm, yeah daddy," YT mumbled while I filled her mouth with my lustful seeds. "Gimme all this sweet nut. Mmmmmm." The fact that she accepted and wanted more of what I had to give intensified my orgasm.

"Ohhhhh shiiiiiiit," I shouted as my body shook and convulsed.

She pumped my dick dry until I went limp, and still, her oral ministrations kept at it.

"OK, OK! Damn ma," I squealed as I pushed her hungry mouth off my tingly dick. A nigga's tip be sensitive as a mutha-fucka after a fat nut. She sucked and sucked and sucked for what seemed like an eternity. Her award-winning mouth's only goal was to draw more semen from me. That shit felt so good I thought I had an out-of-body experience.

"Whaaaa?" YT smiled and wiped the stray drops of cum off the corner of her mouth, then licked her fingers clean. "I love cum. And yours tastes goooooood."

I laughed and shook my head in amazement. YT licked me clean, then put my dick back into my boxer shorts for me. "King, you cool as fuck. I don't care if you have a bitch. I ain't trying to settle down myself, but I would like to kick it and get money with a cool nigga like yourself. I'm digging your drip *and* your dick." YT giggled and licked her lips slowly.

"Girl, you a fool," I said and laughed. I liked how she kept it 100, and her head was A-1.

"I want you to hit me up if you ever need some weight or anything —"

"Nah, ma. I don't be fucking with that meth. Them tweekers are too much for me," I said.

"What? You don't like money? What do you do for a living, King? Do you have a job?"

"Nah, not no more."

"Then how do you get your bread? You a hustler?" YT asked.

"You can say that. I do what I gotta do to be straight."

"That's what's up. I admire that. Do you do any *legal* things for your paper?"

"Hell yeah! I'm a multi-faceted hustler. I have a few endeavors and businesses I'm invested in. They might not be poppin' right now, but I have some legit shit on deck."

"Cool, cool. That means you're no dummy. Most of these niggas out here blow they money at the club and on bitches, but that's 'bout to stop with this Corona shit."

"What chu mean?" I asked.

"King, they about to shut some shit down. Ain't you been watching the news?"

I shook my head. The news was all about tragedy and sadness, so I stayed away from it. I could check the weather on my phone if I needed to.

"Well, whatever the fuck this virus shit is, they about to close a lot of public places, bars included. This was probably our last night here for a while," YT said.

I just looked at her in bewilderment. I was high, and so was she. I figured she was talking out of her ass and overexaggerating. I had heard some shit about a virus overseas, but I didn't think it pertained to us. I just shrugged.

"So you better have a hobby or something to do when they close everything down, cuz you're gonna have to stay your ass at home."

"Girl, you trippin'. Ain't nobody finna be at the crib. And I'm sure they're not closing everything down," I said and shook my head.

"OK, you'll see. Do you be gone a lot?"

"Yeah, I'm never home. There is always a dollar to be made, and I don't care where it's at. I'm going to get it!"

"Ooooh, I love the way you talk! So, tell me some stuff you like to do."

"I ain't gon' lie ma, I'm real versatile. I like to do all kinds of shit as long as I'm having a good time doing it."

"Stuff like what?" YT asked.

"Shiiid, bowling, darts, amusement parks, fishing, dancing *obviously,* shopping, roller skating, cooking —"

"Nigga, you can't cook!"

I then proceeded to name my infamous dishes loved by many.

YT smacked her lips. "Mhm. What else you like to do? What's your biggest passion?"

"Oh, that's easy —writing."

"Writing? What do you write?"

"What *don't* I write is the question. Well, I write poetry, songs, plays, books —"

"Boy, you don't write no books!"

"Yeah, I do." I pulled my phone out and brought up my titles on Amazon.

"Dammmn, that's dope. So how many you got out?"

"Four of 'em. But it's been a minute since I dropped a book though."

"Why?"

"Well, work took ten hours of my day, and I'd be too tired to type. Then with all the other stuff going on in my life, I just don't have the time or the urge to write.

"Well, you about to have plenty of time on yo' hands now."

"Girl, here you go with *that* shit again."

"I'm for real, King. Get in the lab and drop something new." YT said and grabbed my hand.

"I don't know. It's not that profitable for the work I put in, so I just do it when I can."

"I feel you. Whatever's bringing in the most dough gets your time," YT said.

"Exactly! Muthafuckas don't really read no more. They too busy on Facebook and Snapchat. So when I was out there slangin' my books —which are pretty good by the way — not a lot of people were buying. Cheap muthafuckas offer you crumbs for material you invested thousands in. Fuck that. I got plenty books in my garage, thousands of dollars' worth just collecting dust."

"Damn, well muhfuckas finna be home now, so get ready to get that paper you're sitting on. And while you're at it, drop a new joint to entertain the people who ain't gonna have nothing to do *but* read. I know what chu mean. Even though I actually love reading, I ain't got no time to pick up a book. I'm too busy picking up a check."

"Yeah, I'll give it to you on that one. You's a hard ass bitch to fuck with that meth game."

"Man, I'm a crazy bitch, King. You see my nose? It's been broken seven times. Yeah, I like to fight. That shit that popped off in the club tonight? That's my shit!" YT punched her palm. "I would have preferred more blood and or teeth to have come from the punk bitch, but it's aiiiight. We gave they bitch ass some smoke. I live on the edge, man. I need excitement to stimulate my mind, and tweekers bring their crazy A game every motherfucking day bro! But I don't just be moving ice. Yeah, it's my main income, and I actually get a kick out of the shit I see tweekers do, but I'm weird like that. I'm originally from Arizona, and down there, I have the plug on everything. Weed, coke, heroin, molly, or whatever."

"Straight up?" I asked in surprise.

"Yup, and it's all top-shelf shit too. I don't fuck with no bunk work."

"How much for a pound of gas?"

"Two grand, and it's all kinds to choose from."

I looked at YT with dollar signs in my eyes. If she really had the plug like she said she did, I was about to be one rich muthafucka!

"I'm gonna have to take a look at that shit," I said skeptically. She opened her glove box and pulled out three prescription pill bottles, each filled with a different type of weed: Sativa, Indica, and a Hybrid.

"This is the stuff it will be," she said, and handed me the bottles. I pulled the pungent buds from each bottle. I smelled and examined each one. As somewhat of a weed connoisseur, I was extremely impressed by what she had and what we smoked. I told her I needed one ASAP.

"I gotchu Daddy. The first one's on me. Just promise to shop with me if you like the product. Is that cool?"

"Hell yeah, that's cool! Damn, I'm sure glad I came here tonight," I admitted. Sometimes blessings come out of messed-up situations and meeting her was life changing for me.

❧ 7 ❧

QUEEN

I was at a crossroads in life. I came into the new year thinking and hoping for one thing but ended up experiencing another way of life. However, after every storm, there's a pretty rainbow...

"I was hoping you'd contact me. The piece of paper you wrote your information on got misplaced or thrown away by my maid."

"Wait, you have a maid?" I asked.

Koa laughed. "Yes. I have a rather large home, and I don't have the time to keep it clean. But yeah, I tried looking you up on Facebook and other social media outlets. When I typed in Queen, I got all kinds of names. Queen of this, Queen of that, Queen of everything! Do you know how popular your name is?"

I laughed. Oh, I knew. My name was one of those popular titles like "Lil," was with rappers.

A lot of bitches either wanted to be or *were* Queens. I was an authentic one, so I didn't care who the others were. All I could do was be me.

"Yeah, my name means something a lot of women feel like they should be."

"I get it. Everyone wants to be more than what they are," Koa commented.

"Or maybe they name themselves what they aspire to be," I added.

"Hmmm, you have a valid point there."

"Yeah, back to this maid business though. Are you rich or something?"

Koa laughed. "Nah, not really, but I do live comfortably."

"Oh ok. That's cool. Well, I'm glad I reached you. I hadn't heard from you, and —"

"Again, I apologize. Don't think I'm one of those wham-bam-thank-you ma'am —"

I burst out laughing. Koa was so old fashioned it was funny. "I was hoping to see you again before I left, but they were closing down the airports."

"Yeah, I kinda figured that's what happened. This whole Coronavirus is crazy," Koa said.

"Who you telling? The world has officially gone nuts!"

We both laughed, and then he asked me, "Other than that, how have you been, Queen?"

"Well, I've been better, but I'm alive, so I can't complain."

"I hear you on that. Be thankful for everyday God wakes you up, because not everyone does." I thought about Koa's comment. He was right, I'd seen plenty of people in my field not wake up to see another day. Life was short and very unexpectant, so one should be grateful for the time we do have and make the most of it.

"I've thought about you every day, Queen. I've missed you dearly," Koa told me.

"Really? But you don't even know me."

"I know you well enough to know I need more of you. Your conversation, your smell, your taste, your smile, your... mmmmm... I want everything you have to offer, and *more*. I want to marinate in your sweetness and drown in your Queendom."

The nigga was blowing my mind with all that romantic ass

seductive talk. No one had ever spoken to me that way before, and it was making my pussy wet. My nipples were large and in charge, and my head was spinning. *What was he doing to me?*

"Koa, I'm four-thousand miles away. How —"

"Shhhh, don't fight it, Queen. What is distance between two people who can make each other feel the way that we do?"

Koa made me feel desired and wanted. The longing in his voice was equal to my yearning for him. Out of all the men I've dealt with, no one made me feel as special as Koa did. I wasn't trying to fall for another man so soon, but the organic chemistry was so electric, I couldn't resist.

"How are we supposed to make something work, when we can't even travel to see each other?"

"What's meant to be will be. Just go with the flow and let God pave the way."

I knew what he was saying was right but my streak of luck in 2020 was horrible, so any hope for a happy future was fractured at that moment. I told Koa about my surgeries and just the shitty year I'd had, but then he reminded me.

"Yeah, but if you hadn't been through all of that, you would have never gone on a vacation. And we would've never met. See, God paved a way for you four-thousand miles away, where you had the pleasure of meeting a man who will treat you like your name."

I bit my lip and tried to stop my heart from beating so fast. Koa's deep, sexy voice reassured me that our one night of ecstasy was not just a one-time fling. He promised to make me feel the way he did that night, for as long as I'd let him.

☙❦❧

I SMELLED HIM BEFORE I SAW HIM. IT WAS A SEXY, MANLY aroma that made my cookie jar tingle.

"How are you ladies doing?" a thuggish-looking brother asked me and my co-worker as we entered the store. I looked him up and down. He was pretty put together for a roughneck. Ripped designer jeans and an aqua-blue Polo that matched his Air Max 95's. He had a Milwaukee Brewers face mask on. With all of the Coronavirus rules when going out in public, people took to getting customized face masks to make the uncomfortable process a bit more fun. I was just putting my own face mask on before going in.

"If you need anything to occupy your free time, I've got some books here that I wrote —"

"I'm good, sir." I told the thuggish dude who was obviously hitting on me.

"Sir? Damn, I look *that* old?" He joked.

"Um, whatchu mean you wrote a book?" I smiled and tucked my hair behind my ear. He welcomed up to my first refusal and went all in.

"Yo, so I've written these urban novels —"

"Wait, so you actually *wrote* these?" I asked, looking at the books in his hand. I smacked my lips and eyed him suspiciously. Something about him seemed familiar.

"Hmpf, the only thing this... this *person* writes is jail letters," my co-worker commented and pulled me away. I didn't want to make a scene, because she was the head nurse at my job. I apologetically shrugged to the hustler who was visibly hurt behind her comment.

"Can you imagine? *Him*, an author? Ha! Did you see him? He doesn't even look like he can *spell* author!" Heather laughed.

I did see him. He was a little rough around the edges, but every diamond in the rough needed to be polished. Heather went a bit far with the jail letter remark. Ol' boy was definitely not the Fortune 500 type, but that didn't mean he was a convict.

"I don't know Heather. I am needing some new reading materials. What else do I have to do when I'm not working? And who cares if he didn't write the books himself. I wouldn't mind seeing if they're any good," I told her.

"Suit yourself, but if he tries to rob or murder one of us-" I tuned Heather out from there. She was cool, but she was boujee and had her own way of life. I didn't like her any less because of her stereotypical opinions, but damn, that woman knew how to take it to the extreme.

"He looks a little shady, and I know I've seen him around Walmart, selling tickets or DVD's or something."

"Really?" I asked.

"Yes Queen. He looks very familiar. Even with that damn mask on, I recognize him."

I didn't want to tell her he seemed familiar to me too for some reason. It was a nagging suspicion that I had to find out for myself.

We grabbed our bags of goodies and exited the store. I saw Mr. Hustler occupying a young woman with his merchandise. Once he was done with her, I walked up to him.

"You be selling stuff in front of Walmart?"

"Hell yeah. Gift certificates, magazines, gas cards —"

"Ya see? I told you I was right! Let's go." Heather grabbed my arm.

"Go ahead, Heather, I'll be right there."

"Look ma, I don't know what's up with your uptight friend —"

"Uptight? How dare you!" Heather exclaimed.

"Heather, just start the car. I'm coming," I said to my co-worker, who walked away irritated.

"What's her deal? Telling niggas all they write is jail letters and shit. She bogus as fuck."

"Hey, I'm sorry about that. She tends to judge a book by its cover," I said into his eyes.

"Speaking of books." He dug into a Green Bay Packers tote bag and pulled out a few books.

"I have something for all tastes. Hood-crime drama. A coming-of-age love story. A book of poetry. And a contemporary story about kid geniuses that take over the world."

I looked at him and then the books he held in his hand. "And you really wrote all of these?"

"I sure did. It's kinda my thing. Writing is my therapy. Novels, poems, screenplays, music, and yes, even jail letters." He laughed. "I love to write. It's how I clear my head. A friend of mine recently got me back into it, I just wrote this one and dropped it last week." He handed me a book that said *A King Must Have...*

I raised my eyebrow and looked at him. "Wow, and all of these are published?" I asked and grabbed some books out of his hand.

"No, these are all self-published. The big wigs ain't fucking with me. I'm too outspoken and grimy. So I fund my own projects and try to make a dollar out of fifteen cents."

I looked at his titles. *A Bad Boy with A Heart of Gold. In My Feelings. TrapStars & Kingpins,* and *Our Future World.* All of the books had KING written on the bottom of them. "That your author name?" I said, pointing to the book.

"Well, yeah. But it's my real name too. So..."

My eyebrows raised, and I accidently dropped his books on the ground.

"Damn, ma. I have to pay for these ya know?" He bent over and retrieved his books. "Can't really sell them for full price if they all beat up and shit."

"I-I'm sorry. I just..."

"Look, each book is $10. If you just want to check one out to see how my writing game is, I would greatly appreciate it."

"Um, I don't have any cash on me. Do you have Square or Cash App or anything?"

"Nah, I only deal with money ma. Sorry."

"Well, that *is* money. You have to get with the times. People don't carry around cash like that anymore. If you're truly a hustler, you're going to take money in all forms," I told him. The way he looked at me, I thought he was going to snap. His grimace softened, and he handed me two books. *A Bad Boy with A Heart of Gold* and *Our Future World*.

"Tell you what, Miss I-have-no-cash. You take these two books. They're probably more of your speed. If you like them, you can send me $20 on Facebook. If not, keep your money and use my shit as coaster. My social media info is at the back of the books. Is that OK? Cuz I see your girl mean-mugging us over there. She looks like she's about to call the cops on me if you don't get in that car soon." He laughed a deep, genuine laugh that made me giggle too.

"Alright, I can do that Mr. King," I said and began to walk towards the car.

"Hey, beautiful. What's your name by the way?"

I looked over my shoulder as I opened the passenger door. "Queen," I replied as I pulled my mask off and hit him with my own mega-watt smile. I saw his eyebrows shoot up, and a million butterflies fluttered around in my belly. I looked down at the books he gave me and ran my fingertips across his name. *Was he really a King, or was it just something he named himself?* That question alone made me want to find out more about the young writer.

❧ 8 ❧

KING

It was her; eggplant bitch. I didn't know it until she removed her mask, but it was her alright. I couldn't believe she didn't remember me. Maybe because I cut my dreads off and had a face mask on, or maybe she was one of those hoe bitches that hooked up with dudes on the regular, and her conquests were just a sea of forgettable faces. I remember she told me she didn't care what my name was and didn't want to know it. That told me a lot right there. But still, when she got in the car, I was feeling some type of way. *Queen?*

I don't get my nose open over women. A bad chick is a bad chick. *Period.* And shorty was bad. Pussy was bogus as fuck, but **damn**, she was something nice to look at! She had one of those odd noses that I found sexy. But I was trippin' off her name. Was she for real? A lot of chicks called themselves Queen, especially when they found out what my name was, as if the mere fact of them calling themselves Queen would automatically make them *my* royal ride or die sidekick. *SMH.*

I was a bit intrigued though, and I wanted to find out who she was. When I got home, I did some research. I typed in Queen on Facebook and Queen of everything popped up. Queen Bee, Queen Boss Lady, Queen of England. It was hundreds of

Queens. I wasn't about to search through all of those bitches to find out who shorty was. It wasn't like I was trying to fuck or anything. I was completely turned off by what went down between us. I was just curious as to who she was, but I wasn't about to sweat her. If she was feeling my lit, she'd send my bread or get in contact with me. Until then, I was going to keep chasing my paper and doing what I did best.

After growing tired of searching for Queen, I decided to get on POF. It is one of the most-popular dating sites on the internet, and I had gotten plenty of "fish," off that muthafucka. I hadn't been on there in a while because I was going hard writing my new book *A King Must Have...*

I had lots of messages to reply to, so I skimmed through the ones with potential.

A woman by the name of Domeright92 had inboxed me and asked if I wanted to meet up. It was just that easy. Within seconds, we were planning on meeting up where I knew we would hook-up before the day was over. She told me to come to her apartment on the east side.

"Damn, you sexy as muhfucka, ma," I told the pretty chick I was meeting for the first time.

"Why, thank you handsome. Come in," she said, opening the door for me.

I did a quick survey of her place and knew she wasn't the cleanest of women. Dirty clothes were strewn about, the sink was overflowing with dirty dishes, and the whole apartment reeked of cigarettes and stale beer.

"You can have a seat on the couch," she said. I looked at the raggedy corduroy couch with the stuffing busting out of the cushions and shook my head in disgust. *This bitch trifling as hell*, I thought to myself. I sat so far on the edge of the couch that I almost fell on the floor.

"My name is Chandra by the way."

"Hey, Chandra. I'm King," I said, looking her up and down. *How could a bitch this bad live so nasty?*

"Ooh, I love that name. Can I get you anything, King? A drink? Something to eat? Some fire ass head or something?" Chandra said with a mischievous smile.

My eyebrows shot up instantly. *Damn, she ain't waste **no** time. Shorty 'bout that life!*

"Uh, can I use your bathroom quick? Then we can do whatever," I said.

"Sure. It's the first door on your left." Chandra pointed down the hallway.

Now, I already knew she wasn't no housekeeper by how her place was kept, but I *always* look in a person's bathroom to see just how clean or nasty they *really* are. The bathroom is the place of hygiene. It's where you wash your ass, brush your teeth, and get fresh at. So if that muhfucka wasn't right, ten times out of ten, the person whose bathroom it is ain't right either.

Not only were panties and bras laying all over the floor, sink, and bathtub, but she also had sex toys in the sink, bathtub and even in the soap dish! Wasn't no muthafuckin' soap in the bathroom, but a tube of Anal-Ese Strawberry cream sho nuff sat in the damn soap dish. *Really bitch? A bottle of Dial hand soap is a muthafuckin' dolla at the dollar stoe!* Wtf?!

I took one look at the toilet and did an about-face. I couldn't even get fully out of the bathroom before the bitch latched onto me like a centipede.

"Ooh, daddy. I been... mmm, wanting to... " She sucked my lips and licked my face in between confessing her kinky desires to me. "Give you this... hot pussy, since you first, mmm, messaged me. My pussy is leaking right now for you, daddy. So, what's up? You wanna fuck or what?" she looked into my eyes and asked me. Her hand was clutching my dick through my jeans, but I was trying to get back to the living room, where I could breathe and get some air.

Normally, my wood be on full brick if a bad bitch jumped my

bones like she was doing, but my mind was blocking out any physical desire I had for her by broadcasting her uncleanliness to my frontal lobe.

"Uh, look, ma. I can't stay long cuz —"

She cut me off with a kiss and wrapped her arms around my neck. "Daddy, you only need to stay long enough to get us both off, and then you can go do what you gotta do," she said and pushed me against the wall. She dropped to her knees and went for what she wanted.

I looked down at her pretty face as she licked, sucked, and spit on my limp dick. "What's wrong, baby? You wanna smoke or drink first to relax?"

I didn't want to tell her all the smoking and drinking in the world wasn't going to make my dick budge. Her uncleanliness was engraved in my mind, and I couldn't get around it. "Sure, I'll take a drink," I said, trying to be polite.

"I only drink Hennessy, is that cool?" Chandra asked.

"Yeah, that's fine," I replied. As soon as she went to get the Hen, I texted my homegirl Meesha. *AA in 10.* It was our secret code asking for Aid and Assistance from whatever situation we were trying to get out of. All I had to do was stall Chandra for six-hunded seconds...

"Here you go, King. This oughta help you relax. I hope I wasn't coming on too strong," she said, handing me a tall glass full of the strong, brown liquor.

"Nah, you good. Damn, ma, you expect me to drink all this? I won't be able to walk outta here, let alone drive!" I laughed.

"Shiiid, what you don't drink, *I'll* finish," she said and drank from her own tall glass.

"I usually only fuck with Crown."

"Crown Royal?" she said, scrunching up her face.

I wanted to say, *Bitch, do you scrunch your face up like that when you enter your own bathroom?*

"Yes, Crown Royal. Every King must have his Crown."

"Mm-mm. Fuck that whiskey shit. I need this top-shelf Cognac," she said and gulped more.

I sipped the Henny as she made small talk.

"You relaxed yet, baby?" Chandra asked before she straddled me. She pulled her titties out, and those muthafuckas were pretty as fuck! I was wrestling with my conscience by that point. I wasn't trying to fuck ol' girl's nasty ass, but her sexy body was starting to change my mind. That was the longest ten minutes of my life.

If it ain't about the money, don't be blowing me up, nigga I ain't gettin' up...

My ringtone went off. "Hold up, ma. I gotta answer this," I said, pushing her off my lap. She whimpered when I removed her. "Hello? Yeah, what's up? Say what?" I put a shocked tone in my voice and sat on the edge of the raggedy love seat. "Are you for real? A'ight, I'll be right there. Gimme like... twenty minutes." I hung up the phone and looked at Chandra.

"What's wrong, King? Everything OK?"

"Hell naw. My cousin just got beat up real bad. I gotta go."

Chandra stood up and pulled her pink leggings down. She didn't have any panties on, and her pussy was fat as a bitch.

"Damn!" I said out loud.

"Yeah, I wish you could stay to beat ***this*** up real bad," she said and touched her monkey. She turned around and touched her ankles. There was a red lips tattoo on her left butt cheek and some kind of Aztec tramp stamp right above her ass crack. She looked back at me and smiled. "Are you sure you can't stay for a little while?"

"I wish I could," I said and stood up. "But I really gotta get going, ma. I can come back later if you want me too though."

She crawled onto the love seat on all fours. "Damn, my pussy is wet as hell right now. I guess I'll have to take care of myself until you get back."

I heard her talking but couldn't register what she was saying because I was hypnotized by the bottoms of her feet. They were dirty as fuck like she was walking around in charcoal. My dick got hard instantly. *Fuck!* I swore to myself as I pulled the condom out my pocket and made my way towards her. The dirty feet did it for me. It *always* did it for me unfortunately. I don't even like feet, but when I see the bottoms of a bitch feet and they're dirty? It was some kind of weird aphrodisiac for me.

My auntie always told me, "King, if a bitch got dirty feet, she's a dirty ass bitch."

Chandra showed me just how dirty and nasty she was. She let me fuck every hole on her pretty little body. I didn't even take my pants off. I pulled my dick through my zipper and rolled the Magnum on. She was wiggling her butt erotically and flickering her tongue at me. None of that meant a damn thing to me as I stared at her filthy feet and did my thang.

9

MEESHA

"You fucked the bitch, didn't you?" I asked King when I let him into my apartment.

"Huh? What chu talking 'bout?"

"Nigga, you needed AA three hours ago. You ain't answer the phone after I last talked to you, which *means,* you stayed and fucked the bitch didn't you?"

King didn't answer me. He just walked in the kitchen and got a Calypso out of the refrigerator.

"So, what changed your mind? She offer you some money? She get you high?"

"Her feet were dirty," he told me and shook his head.

"King, I love you, but you got issues, boy. You just as nasty —"

"Yeah, yeah, yeah, I know. I don't know what the fuck is wrong with me," King said.

"You're a man. That's what's wrong with you, nigga. Y'all think with your dick."

"Yeah, yeah, whatever. Besides being dirty, she was pretty good though," King said and told me about his latest sexual conquest.

It was like that with him. We had a very open and honest

friendship. We'd been best friends for almost ten years. I knew everything about him, and he knew everything about me.

I'm one of those women that get along better with men than I do with other chicks. A lot of women are bitches and be too much drama for me. I can kick it with the guys without the cattiness and jealous bullshit most bitches be on. The worst thing I had to worry about from a man is him trying to hit on me. I could reject a muthafucka respectfully and show him that I was good company, and an even better friend.

"Don't be calling me for help if you're not gonna use it," I informed him.

"A'ight, Me-Me, damn," he said, calling me the nickname he gave me years back. "Here." King handed me an ounce of loud.

"Bout time you brought me my weed, nigga. Shit, you know a bitch gotta smoke," I said and smelled the potent marijuana. "Dang, this shit is pretty. This ain't your normal loud."

"Nah, remember the native chick I told you about?"

"The one who told you to write a new book?" I asked.

"Yeah, well, she really is the plug. Bitch gave me a pound of wedding cake and showed me all the flavors she can get. Shiiid, I'm 'bout to open up shop for real for real with this," King said.

"Don't be jumping out there too hard King. You got the books going, and what's the word on your lawsuit?"

King had a wrongful termination and sexual harassment suit against his old job. After recording his boss and him, he told her to come up with $100,000 or he would make the tapes public. She offered him $2,000, and he told her to go fuck herself.

At first, they offered him his job back and said they'd pay the lost wages he would've made since he was terminated. He laughed at them and turned them down. His second offer was for $10,000, which he denied as well.

"They up to $50,000 now cuz they see I ain't playing. Thhem muthafuckas been low-balling me the whole time. My lawyer said it would be a long, drawn-out process and that I should just be patient, but shit, I'm trying to get paid ASAP!"

"I heard that. I still can't believe the bitch came at you like that," I said.

"I know, right? Y'all women a trip!"

"Nigga, don't be putting me in the category with all those other bitches. You already know I'm cut from a different cloth."

"Yeah, you're right Me-Me. My bad, ma."

"But you do attract the crazies and wack jobs, so..."

"I attracted you, so what does that tell ya?"

"Bro, that was a hundred years ago. Before I *knew* you. Back when I thought you were a decent guy."

"Ouch," King said and put his hand over his heart like I had just hurt his feelings.

"You know I'm being honest. You're a dog, King. You can't commit to one woman."

"That's because the one woman I would commit to is taken."

I rolled my eyes and sighed. *Not this again.* "King, you wouldn't have a shot in hell with Kim Kardashian, fool. You need to wake up from that dream."

"Shiiid, bullshit ain't nothin.' If Kayne fuck up, I'm sliding to L.A. and shooting my shot."

"Forever the dreamer. I admire your ambition, my nigga," I said, patting him on the shoulder before I headed to the kitchen.

"You want me to roll up?"

"What chu think, fool?" I replied as I poured us some drinks. "I Got this Salted Caramel Crown I'm 'bout to crack open."

"Oooh, I'm ready for that!" King rubbed his palms together excitedly as I set our glasses down on coasters. He began splitting open a Backwoods, and I broke down the weed.

"Damn, this shit's so pretty I don't even wanna smoke it," I commented as I investigated the colorful frosty buds. There were purple, blue, pink, and neon-yellow buds throughout the weed.

"I know, right? This that *real* Cali shit. I need $325 a zip for this shit."

"Dang, man. That's $125 more than normal," I whined.

"Bitch, look at it! You ain't never had no shit like this before. Wait 'til you smoke it," he said as he rolled the blunt.

It smelled like actual cake and was soft as cotton candy. I was excited about trying it but wasn't excited about the extra price tag he was putting on my bag.

"For you I'll do $250, but that's as low as I'm going, Me-Me. You won't run through this stuff so fast cuz it's ten times stronger than my normal gas — "

"For real?" I said, admiring the exotic weed.

"Yeah." King dried the Backwoods, then lit it up. He choked on his first pull, so I knew we were about to have a good smoke session. Whenever King and I got high, we always had interesting conversations and came up with new ideas together. We were a good team.

"How's the new book selling?" I asked.

"Pretty good. The Amazon sales are steady, I'm in the Top 20."

"Ayy, that's what's up! Congratulations." I high-fived King.

"Thanks, ma. The hand-to-hand sells are pretty decent. I'm selling at least twenty a day."

"That ain't bad."

"Hey, it's $200, and I'm not breaking my back doing hard labor."

"I heard that. Your last gig really fucked you up."

"Shiiid, fucked me *over* is more like it," King said and rubbed his arm. Apparently, he had some muscle damage in his shoulder from all the repetitive heavy lifting he did at his last job.

"Your shit still fucked up?"

"Yeah. I got a steroid injection the other day. If this don't work, I'm gonna have to have surgery. I'm not looking forward to that cuz I won't be able to use my arm for like three months!"

"Dang. You better call up your freaky ass fat bitches to take care of your ass then."

We laughed. "Shut the fuck up. I'll make your ass take care of me."

"Yeah right. You finna be laid up doing nothing, which means you gon' be cranky as hell. Uh-uh, I'm good. I'll bring you some food every now and then though."

"Wow, that's how you do a nigga?"

"Fool, you know I'm just talking shit. I got chu."

"You better!" King said and passed me the blunt that was almost gone.

"Roll another one. This shit is da bomb!"

"I told you. This that real Cali shit. The shit these niggas got out here ain't fuckin' wit' dis. Can I get a refill?" King passed me his empty glass, and I poured us some more Salted Caramel.

"So if they at fifty G'z, how long do you think it will be until you get your money?"

"I don't know. My lawyer said it's a long, drawn-out process cuz they're not trying to up that paper. I got them dead to right, so they gonna have to cut the check. But with this Corona shit going on, it's fucking up the process."

"This Coronavirus is a punk bitch! How long is this gonna last?" I asked frustrated.

"I don't know ma. I been watching the news more because of all this, and I don't think it's letting up anytime soon."

I shook my head. "That's crazy."

"Hell yeah," King remarked and fired up the next blunt. "I'm tired of wearing these stupid ass face masks all the time."

"I know, right? At least you got a bunch of them to match your fits."

"Well, you know your boy has to have matching drip from head to toe." King smiled.

I remember when I first met him. It was his pretty ass smile that attracted me to him. King is a dark-skinned brother, but his teeth are as white as the bedsheets he makes women want to roll around in with him.

"Mhm, I know you do. So what's the plan once you get that money?" I asked.

"Pay off any bills I owe so my credit score can go up. Then

I'm getting a food truck so Tee can do his thang."

"Y'all still gonna do the food truck, huh?"

"Yeah. We were supposed to go half on it when he got his taxes back, but I guess they took all his shit for child support, so I'm gonna put all the money up for the truck, food, and licensing and let him run it."

"That's cool. That nigga can cook his ass off, so y'all gonna make a killing," I told King.

"Yeah, I'm trying to get that 'after the bars close' money. That's when muthafuckas be the hungriest when they're drunk and high."

"Mhm, sho' is."

"I almost got all the money together for my shoe store, but with everyone losing their jobs, I don't know if that's a wise investment. What chu think?"

"Yeah, you should hold up until the economy bounces back. Muthafuckas can't go nowhere, so they ain't trying to buy no shoes like that right now."

"Yeah, that's what I was thinking. So many jobs were lost. I don't see how shopping is gonna be a big activity anytime soon. But I'm sitting on all those cases of sneakers."

"Put 'em on Facebook Marketplace or your Snapchat story. The people who *do* have money and want some fresh kicks will scoop them up."

"True, true." King nodded his head and blew weed smoke out his nose. "I got a lot of shit I'm trying to do Me-Me. I know you down for me and got my back, but I need a solid ass team with me if I'm ever gonna do it stupid big like I envision."

"King, you already know I'm with you. I been putting up money for our business venture too, but I'm still a ways away." Me and King were gonna start a Spa for couples. The ladies would be pampered by the best of organic products by sexy as men, and the men would get the royal treatment from some bad ass chicks.

"Yeah, I should have the rest of mine when the settlement

comes in."

"You haven't been pimping none of your fat girls?"

"For the last time, Meesha, I don't pimp. I do *however*," he said with an English accent, "rent out my services."

"Mhm, whatever you wanna call it muthafucka. Have you been hitting their pockets?"

"From time to time. The last bitch damn near killed me she was so heavy!"

"Say whaaaat?" I laughed.

"Yeah, two tons of fun was a wild one. Bitch wanted me to fuck her against the wall. I tried, but she had to be *all* of four-hundred."

I whistled. "Whoa, buddy."

"Yeah, I know, right? But it's all good. Mami pay what she weigh."

"Oh, so you get four-hundred dollars to fuck her?" I joked.

"Nah, she hits me wit' a G."

"She gives you a thousand dollars to have sex with her?" I knew King did his gigolo thing from time to time, but I didn't know he was getting it like *that*. Most of his flings bought him the fly gear he be in, but he was checking they pockets too.

"She sure does. Cash money. And if they're really satisfied with the session, which most of them are, they tip me an extra Franklin or two."

"So you a damn escort now?"

"Mmmmm, if that's what you want to call it. If you ask me, I'd say I'm just a provider of services. I provide you with weed. Others, I provide with dick."

I busted out laughing. "Boy, you on some other shit."

"Hey, these bitches gots to pay to play. Y'all been doing the shit for ages —"

"There you go with this 'y'all' shit again. I ain't never need a man to pay me shit. I'm —"

"An Independent woman. Yeah, I know Me-Me. But you know how bitches is."

"Oh, I know. Some of my homegirls be doing the most. Look, I ain't mad at chu. Get your paper. Just be safe with it."

"Fa sho, you know I will. I don't fuck around unless it's worth it though. Other than that, I'm just trying to run it up."

"As you should. So you ain't meet no women selling your new book yet?" I asked. I was dying to hear some of his juicy new exploits that I knew he was harboring. He was a partyholic and manwhore, *literally*. His adventures made for great listening entertainment.

"A few decent new prospects. Nothing really mind-blowing. But I'll be getting me some new poon soon," King said and laughed loudly.

I giggled too. "I know how you need new ass."

"Hey, I have new-pussyitis. Of course I need new ass!" King exclaimed. *New-pussyitis* is the disease King says he "suffers" from, where he loses interest in a woman as soon as he sleeps with her because the pussy is no longer "new" to him. He says his piqued interest will only hover if he doesn't have sex with a chick. His lust and desire for a woman is only fueled by the knowledge that he's never had her. But as soon as he does? She becomes yesterday's news. It's the bogus shit men do and knowing King has showed me just how men could be.

"The feel, taste, moves, sounds, and passion of a new lover is a euphoric high that no drug can match," he told me some years back, when we debated why men cheat.

"You and your new-pussyitis," I said, shaking my head. "What if you meet that woman with pussy so good you won't want another woman?"

"Not possible. There is no such woman."

"Kim Kardashian?" I said with a mischievous smile.

"OK, OK, maybe there is that one out there to make a nigga not want another."

"Mhm. You're just a dog, King. You hump any and everything and keep it moving."

"Woof woof, muthafucka," he joked.

"Why can't a good bitch find a good dude who don't wanna fuck everything?"

"Cuz a nigga can't find a good bitch that won't fuck off," he spat back.

I rolled my eyes. "King, you know that shit ain't true. You know me. And you done fucked off some good women that was good to you—"

"Yeah, they were good around me, but I wasn't with them 24-7. Ain't no telling what they did behind my back."

"You think everybody is like them bitches that hurt you, King. They're not."

"I prove my theory right every time I fuck a bitch best friend. These hoes ain't shit. Hell, I ain't either, but at least I can admit it."

"I'll give you that, but still. It's wrong all across the board."

"It may be wrong, but I prove myself right every time I do it. Checkmate beeyotch!"

"Fool, whatever. Dang, I'm high as a muthafucka."

"I told you this was that bomb shit!"

I blew smoke rings at the ceiling and thought about King's philosophy. Besides being a dirty dog, he was actually a pretty good human being. He'd had my back more times than I could count, and we had some real-life situations that made us closer. Plus, I liked his brutal honesty.

He was giving, smart, funny, and had that bad boy swag that made bitches panties wet. A lot of men possessed these traits, but did a woman have to settle for what men like King did just to have *some* kind of happiness? That was what polyamorous relationships were about, but I wasn't the sharing kind. Why did I have to share my man with another bitch? *You're doing it whether you like it or not*, King told me one day, and to a degree, he was right. All the guys that cheated on me, gave my dick to another bitch behind my back and left me heartbroken and in tears.

I wasn't trying to settle, but in reality, I ended up doing it every time just so I wouldn't have to sleep alone.

❧ 10 ❧

QUEEN

"Yes, baby, make that pussy squirt for daddy," Koa growled.

I was ramming my vibrator in and out of my dripping pussy while my boyfriend stroked his big, hard dick for me. We both had our laptops out while we masturbated for each other on Skype.

"Ooh, Koa, I wanna see you cum long and hard for me, daddy. Let's both squirt together," I moaned in ecstasy. Who knew Skype sex could be so much fun?

"Yeah? Is that what you want Daddy to do?" Koa growled as the vein in the middle of his forehead protruded violently. Even with his "fuck face" scrunched up in a contorted ball of ecstasy, he was still the sexiest man I've ever dated.

I couldn't believe my one-night fling on vacay would turn into me being head over heels for my bae. We hadn't gotten to see each other face-to-face because of COVID, but through FaceTime and Skype, we found a way to make it work.

Koa greeted me every morning with a good morning text and some kind of Pinterest quote that was either romantic or funny. He sent me flowers and gifts on the regular, and treated me like the Queen that I am. I finally found my fairytale man when I least expected it. What more could a girl ask for?

"Oh shit, I'm getting close, baby, cum with me," Koa said as his fist pumped his member back and forth excitedly. "Let me see that pretty pussy."

I spread my legs for him, and my excitement pooled in the crack of my ass. I was sopping wet. "Mmmm, I'm close too Daddy! Ahh, yesssss." Koa gave me better orgasms long-distance than most men did in person, and fucking with him taught me how to squirt. I used to think I had to pee when that sensitive spot in my ulterior wall got touched, but Koa was like, *keep at it until liquid comes forth*, and that's exactly what I did.

"That's it, baby. Ram it in deep. Fill that motherfuckin' pussy up and squirt on Daddy's dick!" Koa commanded.

"Ohhhhh sh-sh-sh-iiiiiiiiid," I stuttered as the tidal wave of pleasure bubbled to the surface. When you can feel the release ride the escalator of lust, it's a euphoria like no other.

"Pull it out Queen. Pull it out now!" Koa screamed.

I had my eyes closed, but I knew he was nose to camera on the laptop. That nigga's face was all up in the screen, drooling and jagging off to my pretty pussy gushing around that vibrator.

My left hand was trying to rip my burning hot nipple off. When he said pull it out, I yanked the vibrator out and threw it. I heard some crashing noise, but I didn't give two fucks at that point. The orgasm I had was one for the ages. It was like a pleasurable punch in the gut, but deeper. I felt it in my core, was it a soulgasm?

"Koaaaaaaa," I screamed. Spurts of liquid desire gushed out of me like a water hose. The spasms were volcanic bursts of release with each shake. I convulsed, screamed, shook, cursed, blasphemed, moaned, and growled all at the same damn time. A bitch came hard as hell.

"Fuck yeah, Queeeeeeen!"

I opened my eyes and caught the first blast of Koa's seed shoot out of his piece. It went somewhere off camera, probably on the ceiling. Koa stood in front of the camera, and all I could see was from his waist down as he emptied his love for me in his hands in thick spurts.

"Oh yeah. Oh, fuuuuuuck yeah!" Koa chanted.

I raised an eyebrow. His white dude talk during sex killed my vibes sometimes. Koa filled his palm up, and I laid my head on the pillow. I breathed heavily and felt the sweat run down my body. "*Damn,*" we both said at the same time and laughed.

We laid in our beds and talked for another hour before saying goodbye. I sat on the side of my bed and looked at the floor. I knocked everything off my nightstand during my orgasm. No wonder my left hand was hurting. I barely recall it flailing around at some point. From my nipples, to the nightstand, to the headboard, to grabbing the sheets, my hands were everywhere.

I put the stuff back on my nightstand. I saw one of the books I got from 'ol boy at the store. I had been so busy I forgot all about them. Feeling relaxed after a bomb ass orgasm, I propped myself up with a pillow and opened *A Bad Boy with A Heart Of Gold*.

MAY 25, 2020

IT WAS MY FIRST DAY BACK TO WORK AFTER A MUCH-NEEDED three-day weekend. The day started off dreary with the news of Mrs. Sterling's passing. She went peacefully in her sleep on Sunday evening, and I shed a tear for the woman I came to know and take care of.

I decided to listen to my oldies playlist in remembrance of Mrs. Sterling, who introduced me to some classics I had never heard of before her. I remember the ironic feeling I had when I looked at my phone and saw the video.

· · ·

I was borrrrrrn by the river,
    In a little tent.
    Oh, and just like the river I been runnin', ever since.
    It's been a looooong, a long-time coming...

Sam Cooke was singing in the background about change while I watched in horror as a black man was being murdered live by the police. I shed a tear of mourning earlier, and when I watched George Floyd shout, "I can't breathe," a waterfall of anger ran from eyes.

Was this some real shit, or was I watching a fucked-up TV show? When Jenny called me yelling and screaming, I knew it wasn't a dream. It wasn't the first time a black man was killed by the cops, but it was 2020, and the world was already tense enough.

"Them bitch ass, hoe ass muthafuckas!" Jenny shouted. We were FaceTiming each other. "Queen we gotta go up there. You know we got people up there —"

"I was just thinking the same thing," I interrupted her. We spent a lot of time in the twin cities, so we had plenty of people up there.

"You know they 'bout to set it off. We finna let them bitches know we tired of this shit!"

I was with her on that. I wasn't even a violent woman, but there was an "enough is enough" dam that burst through that day. Maybe it was a mix of losing a woman I knew and a brother I didn't know all in the same day. What about the rest of the world though? Were me and Jenny the only ones outraged behind this madness? We soon found out we weren't. I called my girl Sarah, who worked the same houses as me, but a different shift. I told her I was leaving in a couple of hours, and she said she'd cover the rest of my shift.

My phone was blowing up on the way home. Friends and family members from all over the country were saying they were headed to Minnesota. Jenny was going to come pick me up in an hour, which gave me just enough time to shower, change, and pack an overnight bag.

Our nigga Kush, said he would put us up in his crib when we got to the cities, and me and Jenny were on the first thing smoking. It was an hour-drive for us to get to Minneapolis. On the way there, we cried, yelled, and slapped the dashboard every time we swore.

Traffic on the highway was thicker than normal for that time of night. Five miles from our exit, we were at a complete standstill on the interstate. I brought up my GPS maps. The path to our destination was red. What should have been a five-minute drive, registered as a forty-minute delay on my phone.

"Damn girl, it musta been a bad accident up ahead," Jenny said. We looked ahead at the long line of cars at a standstill. That was the one thing about Minneapolis. It was always some kind of construction or something being done on the highway, so I-494 is a clusterfuck most of the time.

I looked at vehicles to the left and right of me. They were full of enraged black faces. People hung out of windows, yelling and holding up handmade signs up and down I-35W.

"Hey, we gotta stop at the store and get some markers and poster board," I told Jenny.

She saw what I was talking about and agreed. "If we can ever get off this damn exit. Shit! Come on, muthafuckas!" Jenny honked her horn long and hard. That triggered a ripple effect of honking cars that seemed to go on forever.

By the time we got off the exit on Lyndale Ave South, we could tell this was no ordinary day in Minneapolis. Cars lined the street in an overwhelming fashion. Men, women, and children were outside in big groups.

"Dang girl, it's 'bout to go down in this muthafucka," Jenny said as we pulled up to Kush's.

"Yeah, I get that same feeling, girl," I said and shook my head.

"Damn, how many muthafuckas do this nigga got over here?" Jenny said as we got out of the car.

Kush owned an upstairs-downstairs duplex in the heart of the city. There was a bedsheet on the lawn that two women were spray-painting, and at least a dozen people chillin' on the porch. Well, chillin' isn't exactly the word I'd use.

"Fuck 12!"

"We gonna show them pigs what's up!"

"Bitch ass police!" The people lounging on the lawn and porch were saying. Guns were being loaded, knives were being sharpened, and signs were being made.

"There go my homegirls!" Kush yelled from the upstairs window, and we looked up and waved. "Come on up, y'all," he said.

We nodded and waved at the people we passed on our way upstairs. Kush Krinkle was a good friend of ours. He raps, produces, hustles, flips houses, and does all kinds of other things. He's what I like to call a "jack-of-all trades."

"Queen! Jen-Jen! What it do?" Kush said and greeted us with big hugs.

"Not much, man. We just came up here to contribute to the cause. We see you got plenty of muthafuckas here already though. You sure you got room for us?" Jenny asked.

"Of course, ma. Y'all got the two bedrooms up here. Everyone else is here for the meeting."

"Meeting?" I asked.

"Yeah, we're planning to execute some order around this bitch! We're gonna start with a peaceful protest, but you know them honkies ain't gonna like that —"

"Uh, you do know there are dozens of white folks in your crib, right?" Jenny asked.

"Yeah, them my muhfuckas tho. I'm talking about them honky cops! And we gon turn it up a notch until we get the results we want," Kush clarified.

"And what's that?" I inquired as I looked around. There were weapons, bullets, hammers, drills, pipe bombs, and all kinds of shit scattered throughout the living room.

"We want all the officers involved arrested immediately! Every one of them pigs that stood around and watched as that racist cracker killed George Floyd. If they not trying to indict and hang those muhfuckas, we gonna set it off in this bitch!"

"Hell yeah. I'm with you on that, Kush," Jenny said.

"That's what's up, ma. Excuse my lack of hospitality. Y'all want something to drink or eat?"

We both said we'd take some water and he brought us a couple bottles of Fiji.

"Whatever you need us to do Kush, we're with you," I said after a sip of water.

"Hey Jenny, this is my homeboy, King —" Kush began to introduce me, but I cut him off.

"Yeah, I know her, bro," I said.

"Huh? Where you know me from?" Jenny rolled her head and stared at me weirdly.

I sighed. "Never mind. It's all good. Kush go 'head, fam."

"OK, so listen. I want y'all to be his eyes and ears. The team of brothers that's about to be on the front line gonna need some women to record they every move. The police gonna rough the men up, but they can't fuck with y'all too much physically —"

"Unless she's 'wee-ooh-wee-ooh-we, wee-ooh-wee-ooh-we, Mrs. Officer'," I said and laughed. Then I saw her. She was on her phone when Kush was talking to me and Jenny, but when she walked up to us, she froze.

"Yeah, the women cops can, but for the most part, all of those policemen will not be able to withhold their aggression, and we want y'all front and center when the shit goes down!" Kush punched his palm and gritted his teeth. "We got phones, cameras, night-vision goggles —"

"Damn, my nigga, for real?" I interjected.

"Mhm. Shit, we got some high-tech artillery on deck fam."

"So you want the females to record the niggas confronting the police?" Queen asked Kush, but she was looking at me. I returned her stare with my own hidden gaze.

"Correct." Kush nodded.

"Kush, we ain't tryin' to just be no side-line bitches. We wanna bring it to their ass too!"

"Oh, y'all gon' get chor chance to bring it, ma. But for our first demonstration, we just need y'all to look good and push record. Can you do that for me?"

"You promise we gon' get to tear some shit up?" Queen asked.

Kush laughed. "Yes, Queen. Y'all gonna have your way in a minute."

"Bet. Count us in. When are we starting?" Jenny replied for the both of them.

"Soon. We're gonna go to third precinct and tell 12 a thing or two," Kush said and winked. "King, give them the rundown while I go holler at Tone and nem," Kush told me.

"This world is small as a muthafucka," I said to Queen after Kush walked away. She batted her eyelashes and looked at the floor. "Hmpf. I don't know about *you*, but I sure don't know any Queens who don't keep their heads up." Immediately, she looked at me, and the look in her eyes was priceless.

"So, how you know my guy Kush?" Queen asked me with nothing but sassiness in her tone.

"Uh-uh, fuck all that. How do you know *me* my nigga?" Jenny pushed Queen aside and got in my face.

"Damn yo, save all that hostility for the protest. I, uh... if you don't remember me, then I guess I wasn't worth remembering," I said and shrugged.

"This is ol' boy I was telling you about that wrote them books," Queen said.

"Ohhhh, OK. *King*. I thought Kush was saying *Cane*. But OK. What chu need us to do boo?"

I shook my head and broke down how we were going infiltrate the police station.

"Damn, y'all really finna run up in the precinct?" Jenny asked, shocked.

"Hell yeah. This da station them four bitch ass cops worked at. If that's they home base, we 'bout to bring it to their home!" I looked at the women and could see the fear in their eyes. They weren't expecting *this* shit. They swallowed the lumps in their throat and poked their chests out.

"Hey, y'all, I need everyone in the living room," Kush announced to us. We walked into the packed front room. People were standing shoulder to shoulder, and lots of chatter was going on.

"Alright, y'all, people have already started taking to the streets. We gotta go," Kush stood on the table and announced.

Everyone filed out of the house. People got in vehicles, motorcycles, skateboards, dirt bikes and many other forms of transportation.

I stood on the porch and could see hundreds of people marching for miles. It was pitch-black out, but the fire torches carried by the protestors lit up the sky with dancing flames that moved in unison. Cars crowded the street with people hanging out of the windows, holding signs and yelling, "Justice for George!" I looked behind me, and Queen and Jenny had cameras around their necks and were ready for me to move.

We walked down Washington and Third, joining hundreds of other people who were tired of the systematic racism and blatant disregard for human life. People of all races and colors walked in unity for one cause... justice for George.

"When I say Black lives, you say matter," I shouted in my bullhorn. "Black Lives!"

"Matter!" The crowd of people surrounding me yelled in unison.

"Black Lives!"

"Matter!"

"Black Lives!"

"Matter!"

My backpack was loaded with all kinds of essentials needed for our mission. It was heavy, but I wasn't complaining. I was running on anger, adrenaline, and alcohol. That was *my* triple A.

By the time we got to Nicollet and 4th, we joined hundreds of white protestors who were already sweating the 5th Precinct with their own outrage. They had their own themes they were communicating.

"Silence is violence."

"Silence is Compliance."

"White Silence is Violence," were all the chants and signs of that group that I told to ride with us. Now we had people of all kinds ready to bring it to the police like they did to us. They marched arm in arm and hand in hand with my team.

Queen walked on my left, always a couple steps ahead, as she filmed the march from my peripheral. When the sky grew dark, my **BLACK LIVES MATTER** hoodie glowed in the dark. It was made to look like constellations in the sky. When I pumped my fist or waved my arm, it looked like shooting stars zig-zagged in the air.

The walk was long, but the closer we got to our destination, the larger our team grew. I looked behind me and saw thousands of people for miles and miles. People fed up with the bullshit filled 26th Ave South. People with hurting hearts. People with empathetic souls. People with plenty of pent-up aggression in their systems and had some shit they wanted to get off their chest *anyway*. People who were just on lockdown for months and never knew what isolation was until the Corona showed them. Once-sane people that lost their muthafuckin' minds because of the once-in-a-life-time fuckery they were *forced* to deal with. I definitely needed those kinds of ticking timebombs to detonate our targets. Rule number two in war; there is strength in numbers.

Kush assigned me a tech guy named Gabe. He was a short,

chubby, baby-faced, hippie-looking dude that was smart as hell. He had the police's frequency and monitored 12 through their own scanner. He was able to listen to their direct conversations and get the exact location of each person speaking. He also had some James Bond tech gadgets for me.

"King, they have a strike team guarding the perimeter, a SWAT Team on the roof, and state troopers blocking off Snelling Ave," Gabe shouted in my ear as he struggled to keep up with me. Gabe was a rotund little butterball. It was funny watching him sweat rivers as he walked on my right side. His hair was matted to his face, and he breathed heavily.

"You OK, Gabe? Ya can't really slow down right now, but as soon as we get there, you can take a seat somewhere," I shouted in his ear.

"No man, I'm OK. I've never walked this much... but... but... I sure do need it!" He huffed.

I patted the chubby hipster on his back. The man had heart, and I admired his desire for self-improvement. He had guts too, he wore a BLACK LIVES MATTER shirt that said *Fuck 12* on the back. It stuck out against his pale skin, which was even more ironic. Gabe carried a laptop, an iPad, and two cellphones in his hands. He worked them simultaneously and communicated with other members of the team. The man was a tech guru.

"So, they got SWAT on the roof, huh?" I asked Gabe.

He swiped the iPad and brought up a live image for me. "This is from our drones. As you can see, they have three quarters of the roof secured." Gabe held the iPad in front of me and zoomed in on the rooftop of the 3rd Precinct. The unmistakable figures in black kneepads, helmets, and assault weapons let me know that yes, it was indeed SWAT. Knowing that they didn't have the roof completely surrounded gave me a strategy for when it was time.

"Here, King." Queen pulled a bottle of water from my backpack and poured it in my mouth as I walked. The cold H2O nourished my parched soul and gave me a revitalizing lift.

"Thanks, ma."

"You're welcome, King!" Queen shouted and began recording again.

"Black Lives!" I shouted and pumped my fist as I saw the precinct up ahead.

"Matter!" Thousands of people behind me shouted.

"Black Lives!"

"Matter!" The powerful echo of all those passionate voices sent chills down my spine. As Minnehaha Ave morphed into East Lake Street, Gabe put a Bluetooth in my ear and said he'd feed me communication from various sources through that. He veered right to take his position.

"Jail All Racist Killer Cops"

"Silence Is Murder"

"Justice! Now!" were the signs and chants in front of the 3rd Precinct. Their bitch asses had already put up a gate to block the front entrance, but that meant nothing to us. We were gonna run up in that bitch!

I walked up the front steps and got on my bullhorn. "We've stood by long enough, law enforcement. Since you feel like black lives don't matter, we're gonna show you muthafuckas that youuuuu don't matter!" I shouted to the barricaded front entrance and threw a rock. It cracked a wooden board they had placed in the windows.

My young goons spread out and made sure the precinct was surrounded. Jenny and a couple of people went around back and padlocked the gate. It was the police's only exit, and we planned to corner them in. They used the same chain that belonged to Blu, the pit bull that was killed by a 3rd Precinct cop a few months back.

I pushed the Bluetooth piece in my ear until I got to the police radio transmission. The sharp crackling of distortion made me wince.

"They are swelling to astronomical proportions. There isn't many in

the back yet, but if we get any more, it's going to be hard for our escape route."

Hearing that let me know that they were going to heed to our demands. We called and told them that we were gonna take over their headquarters and they could either stay or leave.

"Is anyone copying this?"

"I need to know who's in charge of the detail at the 3ʳᵈ Precinct."

"Someone on the Lake Street side has bolt cutters and a torch. They are compromising the fence. I repeat, oh shit..."

I heard male and female voices radioing each other while I stood on the railing of the 3ʳᵈ Precinct and took in the scene. Queen was on the first step, capturing every moment. She put a Black Lives Matter face mask on because fire and smoke were everywhere.

I CAN'T BREATHE and 12 Ain't Shit were the two signs closest to me. I pointed to them, and Queen followed my direction and captured it on video.

My little nigga, Mr. Risk Taking, rode up on a dirt bike and held a burning bottle over his head. He launched the Molotov cocktail at the precinct and did a wheelie on his bike. When the glass exploded and the wooden boards caught fire, he shook his dreads back and forth excitedly and pumped his fist in the air.

"Strike team four members, return to your vehicles."

"But they're throwing pipe bombs and other explosives."

"We are being hit with bottles and rocks, you name it. Permission to use CF?"

*"No tear gas. That will only enrage the issue. You are authorized to use CS Triple chasers **only**, but at your discretion."*

"Guys, we gotta move! We gotta move!"

I could hear the frantic tones in their voices. It was time to make them retreat.

"PB Squad, unite!" I shouted in the bullhorn. Fifty men and women with high-caliber paintball guns emerged from the crowd and went around back where they fired at the police in the rear lot.

"There is a mob of them. Rocks, bottles, bricks, and paintballs are being directed at officers in the back."

"How is it inside the precinct? Base 3, I repeat, is the inside clear?"

"You are authorized to use CS Triple chasers to push that crowd back."

"We would, but uh... we don't have any."

"Demo crew, unite!" I shouted into the bullhorn.

A dozen people with sledgehammers, saws, axes, drills, and demolition jackhammers came to the forefront and went to work. In no time, they had defaced the 3rd Precinct. The gate was torn down, and the wooden boards were shredded up chips of wood scattered on the concrete.

"They've breached the Northwest corner of the fence."

"They're coming in. I repeat, they are coming through the front doors."

"Is there anyone on the roof of the 3rd Precinct who can give me some information?"

"Copy, this is AR-278. It appears they are coming in through the back as well."

"Cleeeeear!" An ex-Navy SEAL named Stanley, yelled. I knew what time it was, and I took cover.

BOOM!

Stanley fired a grenade launcher through the front entrance. A ball of fire ignited and spread to everything flammable. Dust and debris wafted into the air in thick clouds of dust as everything came tumbling down. Glass, brick, and cement crumbled into rubble, and I stepped on a mound of debris like I was pitching in the World Series.

"No justice!" I shouted in the foyer of the police department with one fist high in the air. My immediate team was right behind me in a menacing fashion.

"No peace!" They shouted to the line of cops in riot gear posted on the stairs.

"They're through our front door. They've fired some sort of missile or something!"

"No Justice!" I shouted.

"No peace!" Thousands of people behind me shouted.

I looked at the dozen or so officers in shielded helmets and heavy body armor. As bad as I wanted to shoot them dead, I came to deliver a message that would live with them and the entire world for decades to come.

"Black Lives!" I yelled at the police not even five feet away from me.

"Matter!"

"Black Lives!"

"Matter!" The echo from the people in the front entrance with me resonated powerfully.

"They're shooting mortars at us. They are shooting from a distance of about maybe seventy-five to a hundred yards. We can't reach them. Can we escalate our use of force to deploy scatter rounds?"

"Negative on the scat rounds. I repeat, negative on the scat rounds. There's another plan in place. Standby."

"What plan? We have to act now! They have breached the precinct from all angles."

We had a team of muthafuckas in the Auto Zone parking lot across the street, and people on the roof of the Minnehaha Liquor Store kitty-corner from the 3rd Precinct.

BOOM! Another grenade was launched at the section of the roof where no SWAT were. This took away their exit route and left a wall of flames for them to battle.

"This is SWAT official-451. The roof has just been bombed. We need an exit route pronto."

I could hear all of the communication between law enforcement in my right ear. I looked over at Queen. She pulled her face mask under her chin and screamed and cussed out the police. Her pain and anger were equally matched by all of us who wanted justice for George.

"We want every muthafuckin' officer who was on the

scene prosecuted. They let that murdering bitch Derek Chauvin kneel on our brother's neck while he pleaded for his life. What the fuck does I CAN'T BREATHE MEAN?!"

"I CAN'T BREATHE!" My team behind me shouted.

I threw a bottle at an officer and shouted, "No Justice!"

"No peace!"

"We have a man in a black hoodie, wearing a backpack and talking in a bullhorn in the foyer. He appears to be the ringleader. Permission to take him down?"

"Take me down? I dare you pigs to do something to me. Bring it, 12!" I hurled a chunk of cement at them, and it hit one of the officers in the neck.

"Negative. We are ordered to abort. I repeat, everyone is to evacuate immediately."

"Tou Thao, J Alexander Kueng, and Thomas Lane, *hmpf,* all you muthafuckas are responsible for George Floyd's death. You have his blood on *your* hands!" I said.

"We need to move now. Evacuate! Evacuate!"

"Live debris coming in from all angles."

Wherever a fire was lit, debris, wood, and lighter fluid were thrown on the flames to keep it burning. The once-barricaded headquarters was infiltrated by me and my team. Lake Street and Minnehaha Ave were filled with people holding signs, fists, phones, and torches in the air.

"I'm finishing clearing the building."

"We need to go. As of right now we can leave southbound, we're going to lose that opportunity in about 30 seconds."

We brought the drama from all angles, but we did it without using lethal force. Bottles, sticks, and bricks were lightweight assault weapons.

"We gotta go. We are sitting ducks here. They're about to breach the back gate."

They didn't know the meaning behind the chain and sheet draped over the back gate. The face of a bluenosed pit was spray-painted on the bedsheet. It was Blu, coming back to haunt them in the afterlife.

"I can't get the gate open. It's been padlocked from the outside. They have us trapped in."

"They have blocked our visuals by covering the back gate with a bedsheet."

"Oh my God it can't be. It's... it's Blu!"

"Excuse me? What was that Officer?"

But there was no further response from that cop. All I heard was a loud, deranged scream in my earpiece and a loud bang.

Squad cars burst through the back gate and gave cover to the cops on foot.

"We're intermixed with the cops on foot, trying to give them a fighting chance here."

"The 3rd Precinct has been compromised."

The back gate was rammed open by a squad car. The sheet with Blu's face on it blew onto the windshield as the cops' SUV sped down the street. Other officers ran behind that squad car as mortars, pipebombs, firecrackers, and piss-filled bottles were hurled at them.

"It seems like the precinct is on fire."

"We are evacuating right now. All officers are taking cover."

The line of police vehicles that retreated from our assault was comical. They rode bumper to bumper and were pelted with eggs, paintballs, and everything else under the sun. The officers who fell like white women in scary movies were kicked and spit on. They didn't stay down too long as they got up and ran for their lives.

"King, they're leaving. All of 12 is heading northbound down Snelling," Gabe said into my Bluetooth.

"Dispatch, I think you can start your roll call."

"Bring a couple more squads up to the front. We're going to convoy our officers safely to the... uh, new staging location please."

"They are attacking the squad cars. These people are savages!"

"Hey, y'all. Remember this as the night we made the law run,"

I spoke into the bullhorn. "For George!" I pumped my fist in the air.

"For George!"

"Now tear this muthafucka up!" I said and jumped off the mound of debris.

Hundreds of people ran up in the police station and vandalized the place from top to bottom. Spray cans, baseball bats, hammers, pipes, and two-by-four's, were used to express their pain and anger.

I ran outside and joined my young goons on the front steps. They wore bandanas and baseball caps as they threw up signs and said, "Fuck 12" to their camera phones. I stood on the railing and felt somewhat vindicated. We held bats and blunts in the air, blowing smoke into the flames that shot out of the Precincts windows. Fists were raised in triumph. Chants of all kind was the soundtrack of the streets that night.

Buildings burned all around me for miles. Auto Zone, Target, and Cub Foods were being looted and burned while I watched a city in chaos. It was a symbolic victory for us, and the beginning of reckoning for the rest of the nation.

❧ 12 ❧

QUEEN

They say a man in uniform is an aphrodisiac for most women. Personally, I could give two shits about the uniform. My disliking for the "boys in blue" might have something to do with why I didn't care for the authoritative uniform type.

As much as I loved my boyfriend, Koa, watching King in action ignited tug-of-war with my feelings. Koa was everything a woman could ever dream of. He was tall, dark, handsome, smart, funny, responsible, financially secure, and great in bed. The one thing he lacked was the thing that drew me to the players and fuckboys who broke my heart and shitted on me my whole life.

Bad Boys. The look, the walk, the talk, the tattoos, the swag... bad boys turned me into putty when I absorbed their essence. Koa was a contemporary gentleman. Someone respectful and honest and loyal. So why was I yearning for him to go hood on me and be my Lucious Lyon?

After we set the 3rd Precinct on fire, we were supposed to go downtown, but I had to FaceTime Koa so he could see for himself the mayhem that was going on.

"Hey, baby! Forgive me if I'm yelling in your ear, but I'm kind of in the middle of a protest right now," I said and smiled at my Samoan King.

"Oh my God, Queen. Honey, are you OK?" he asked in a concerned voice.

"Yeah, daddy. I'm good. We just out here taking it to the police!"

"Wooooohoo! Fuck the police!" someone leaned over my shoulder and said to Koa.

I stood next to a smoldering bus shelter because it was the only place that wasn't swarming with people. I lifted my phone in the air and rotated it for Koa to see.

"Bae, the city is on fire. The police have run. There are millions of people on the street."

"I know. I've been seeing it on the news. Speaking of which, young lady, I saw a certain *someone*," he cleared his throat and continued, "in the front of the mob at the precinct. Woman, you almost gave me a heart attack!" Koa said.

"Shut up, for real? Awww shit. How did I look? What did —"

"Queen! Why are you worried about how you look when the whole world saw you take over an entire police precinct?"

"Um, first of all, you ain't seen me do nothing but record my people while they protested, thank you very much," I smacked my lips and rolled my eyes at him.

"Whatever. You're on the news —"

"Good, Koa. I'm glad I'm on the muthafuckin' news. They done killed another defenseless black man in cold blood. So do you think I give a fuck about what they see me doing? Is anything I'm doing worse than kneeling on a man's neck for eight motherfucking minutes? Hell naw it ain't. So, don't be sweating me about no news shit. I'm in this movement, up to my eyeballs in real-life drama, but I'm down for the cause."

"And I admire your tenacity, Queen. March, speak out, let your voice be heard. I'm just asking that you be careful sweetheart. I don't want anything to happen to my Queen."

"Awww, bae, ain't nothing gon' happen to me. I'm surrounded by friends who will do whatever to make sure I'm good."

"Ok, that's good to hear. Well, before you go to sleep, shoot me a text, hun," Koa said.

"I will Daddy. Talk to you later. Bye." I blew a kiss and hung up the phone. Koa was sweet and he meant well, but I knew he didn't feel as strongly as I did for the BLM movement. I mean, he was half-black, so he *should* care, but I didn't see him as the activist type.

I called Jenny to see where she was. I had snuck away to talk to Koa and gather my thoughts for a second. During our conversation, the crowd swelled tremendously as people came from all directions to contribute to the chaos.

"Girl, we in Target loading up some shit. I'm getting us some make-up and perfume and shit. I... hey, bitch, that's my cart! Queen, meet me at the front of Target in five-minutes," Jenny yelled into the phone before she disconnected.

I had to push through the heavy crowd just to get to Target. The familiar shopping store looked like a giant bonfire. Flames and black smoke shot from the rooftop while people ran in and out of the shattered windows. Those plastic red carts of Targets were filled with merchandise of all kinds and pushed by hundreds of people in the parking lot.

"Queen! Queen!" Jenny yelled my name and waved her arms over her head.

"Girl, you crazy. We gotta go," I said, taking her hand.

"I know, I know, but I couldn't pass up the opportunity to get some free stuff. Shiiiid."

I shook my head and radioed King with the walkie-talkie he gave me. "King, this is Queen 91. Give me your location. Your film team is in route."

"I hear you Queen, we are on our way to Max It Pawn Shop, meet us there," King said.

"I gotchu King. Max It Pawn Shop. On my way," I said into

the walkie talkie. We were a few minutes away, but the streets were full of so many people, it looked like a Fairgrounds.

The pawn shop was across the street from the Library which was being shattered piece by piece. Protestors threw rocks and softballs at the artisan-etched windows. The Cesar Pelli — designed Library was one of Minneapolis's most-popular hangouts.

"Queen, look, they hitting the bank, girl. We gotta get some of that!" Jenny exclaimed. As soon as she said that, three squad cars made a sharp left on South 28th Ave and pulled up in front of US Bank.

"Shit! We gotta get King out of the Pawn shop. Come on," I grabbed Jenny's hand and ran across the street. People loaded up cars full of the pawn shops goods as they ran in and out.

"King! King! We're here," I announced loudly, waving my hands over my head. He was busy spray painting a message on the back wall. I pushed record and walked up to him. "We're here King. You need me to do anything?"

He glanced over his shoulder and smiled. "Just keep doing what you're doing now ma."

"Okay!" I was so pumped and excited to be documenting history in the making while letting my voice be heard at the same time.

Boom! A loud explosion was heard in the near distance, and it rocked the whole building. The lights went out, and there were screams in the dark. I lost my balance and put my arm out to keep myself from falling.

"Shit!"

"What the fuck was that?" I heard voices say.

"Is everybody OK? Is anyone hurt?" King asked. Everyone responded that they were good.

King put on some night-vision goggles and told me to keep the cameras flash on while he went back to his "art."

When King finished his graffiti, he took a step back and put his hands on his hips. I zoomed in on him admiring his work, and then I panned out and captured the fresh message on the wall.

Everything In Here Belongs To <u>US</u>!
   Fuck 12!!!
   BLM

"Hey, y'all. We gotta go. They done blew up the bank, so you know they coming," Jenny said.

"I don't think they gonna fuck with us here. They'll be focused on the bank and Western Union next door," King said. "Plus, I'll hear when they're coming on the scanner."

"Whose is that?" I pointed to the Hoverboard box on the floor. The *Swagtron T882evo* was a cool, Lithium-free hoverboard that lit up a rainbow of colors while riding it. I always wanted to get one after learning how to ride my little cousin's one at a family reunion.

"It's yours now," King said. He picked the box up and handed it to me.

"Thank you, Ki —"

"Evacuate now! This is the police. You are trespassing on private property," a voice from outside said. I looked up and saw people jumping out of the windows and running in all directions with arms full of merchandise. Pairs of cherries and berries flashed outside on the sidewalk. I saw a handful of officers enter the pawn shop, spraying mace.

"Take the back exit, Queen. Go!" King urged.

I didn't want to leave him, but I also didn't want to defy him. He oozed the type of authoritative power that I admired and respected, so I did what he said. I pulled the hoverboard out the box and got on it. ***Zrrrrr.*** I took off toward the storage room but didn't get far. There were so many empty boxes and other garbage on the floor, I couldn't ride my new

Swagtron because the stockroom had been completely decimated.

I put my hoverboard under my arm and hopscotched over shelves that were pulled down, broken flat-screen televisions, and all kinds of garbage that lay in the middle of the floor. I heard another loud bang, and this time, I *did* fall face-first into a pile of boxes.

I looked toward the exit and knew I wasn't going to be able to get past the barricade of debris blocking the door. I got up and ran back upfront.

"Stop resisting!" an officer yelled at King as he tased him.

"Heyyyy, get off him, motherfucker!" I screamed and pushed record.

"Ma'am, get back. You are interfering with police business," the cop said and pointed his taser at me.

"Fuck your police business, and fuck you too!" I swung my hoverboard like a baseball bat and knocked the policeman's helmet off.

His taser fell, and King reached for it. I swung the Swagtron one more time and connected with the cops open face that crunched on contact. Blood sprayed in the air like a water fountain. I dropped the hoverboard and hopped on it.

"We gotta go, King, come on," I announced making a clear path toward the front.

"Bitch ass pig, you wanna tase me? I'm immune to this shit! Let's see how *you* like it. Huh? How's it feel, muthafucka?" King said between gritted teeth.

The cop that I knocked out was on his back, screaming while King discharged the taser into his body. The cop wore body armor, so King put the stungun to his exposed neck. "You're lucky it's not my knee like your boy did George." He pulled the trigger until there was no more juice left in it. Once it stopped sparking, King stepped on the officer's chest and followed me outside.

There was only one police car idling on the sidewalk. The

other cops abandoned the pawn shop just as quickly as they got there. The lone "Supercop" who stuck around to exact order and discipline got served a can of whoop-ass real good.

"King, Queen, get in!" Kush shouted from the police SUV.

I don't know where he came from, but boy was I glad to see him. King got in the front and I hopped in the back. Kush turned the sirens on and took off down Lake Street.

"Nigga, where you been?" I leaned over the seat and asked Kush.

"Shiiid, we hit the bank," Kush said and pointed next to me. I didn't notice all the US Bank money bags piled on the backseat until he made me aware of them.

"Dammmmn, all of these are filled with money?" I asked but was looking out the window as we passed burning building after burning building.

"Yup. I don't know how much we got, but we're straight now," Kush said and gave King some dap.

"Hell yeah, that's what's up!" King said. "Fam, please tell me you got some weed. I'm all out and stressing like a muthafucka."

"My nigga, you know I got it on deck," Kush said and handed King a pack of Backwoods.

"Shiiid, I ain't never smoke in a cop car, but I'm 'bout to cross that off my bucket list," King said and lit the fat blunt up.

"I never been in a cop car, but this muthafucka is nice," I commented as I looked around the spacious SUV.

"I know, right? This is one of those new Police Interceptor Utility vehicles," Kush stated. "Get the fuck out the way!" He yelled out the window and honked the horn. People saw a police car driving down the street and threw bricks and bottles at us. Kush hung halfway out the window to let people know that this cop car was being driven by a civilian.

"Queen, where is Jenny at?"

"Shit, I don't know. She was the one who warned us to get out of the pawn shop. I haven't seen her since," I said and tried calling her. "It's going straight to voicemail," I said, a bit worried after getting no answer. "Are there any chargers in here? My phone's about to die."

"Apple or Android?" King asked holding up two chargers.

I told him I was an Apple girl.

King sighed. "Figures... here." He handed me the iPhone USB adapter, and I plugged it into the rear console.

"Figures, what? Huh, King? What's that supposed to mean?"

"Nothing. Never mind."

"Hmpf, whatever, nigga. I just saved your ass." I reminded him.

"I wasn't worried about dude. I had his ass."

"Mmmmmhm, if you say so, King."

"Ok you two. Enough of the husband-wife quarrel. We have to link back up with the team."

Kush sped down the street, driving mostly on the sidewalk. Every few seconds a loud thud would ricochet as another object put dents in the cop car we were in.

I heard King dial a number on speaker phone as I stared dumbfoundedly out the window at the entire city on fire. Smoke, flames, and fireworks lit up the sky, and we were still a month away from the 4th of July.

"Gabe, this is King. Can you give me your location?"

"Yes. We are on the Interstate. We're on I-35W and ready to execute BLM number three."

"Copy that, Gabe. Me, Kush, and Queen are in route now. Let the team know," King said.

"Roger that, King. Safe travels, and we'll see you guys soon," Gabe said and hung up.

A few seconds later, my Snapchat rang. "Girl, where you at? You OK?"

"Hell naw! I lost my muthafuckin' phone wrestling with the police. This one chick let me log onto her snap so I could call you. We 'bout to run up in T-Mobile right now. I need me a phone!"

"A'ight girl, do what chu gotta do. You always losing yo' damn phone. Look, we're on our way to the bridge now. If you can, meet us there. Stay in contact with me and let me know you're ok," I told my BFF.

"Alright ma, you do the same, and take care of that strong brotha we been rolling with."

I looked up front. King was blowing weed smoke at the passersby. I could tell that his genius mind was hard at work, and it made my heart skip a beat. I don't know if it was the adrenaline, the situation I was participating in, or a little bit of both, but I was having feelings that I knew I shouldn't be having. "Oh, I will. You can count on that!"

❧ 13 ❧

KING

I met Kush in a small, hick town jail. He was a blood from the east coast that always repped his flag everywhere he went. I was up in the boonies, fucking with a new sub when we went out and got shitfaced at a redneck bar. They didn't have Uber's or Taxi's up those ways, so when the bar closed, ol' girl chose to drive us back to her crib.

I was drunk as a skunk from Crown Apple and tequila shots. She drank vodka and a half dozen Bloody Mary's that night. I passed out during the drive and woke up to her screaming. When I opened my eyes, her Volkswagen Atlas SUV had veered off the road. The truck did flips in the air before rolling over several times in a ditch.

I was on parole at the time, so I knew it wouldn't be pretty when the cops showed up and saw my current state. I called one of my bitches to come get me, but the hoe was so slow that the cops showed up before she did. I couldn't run because it was pitch-black out and we were in the middle of nowhere. There weren't any streetlights for miles, just acres and acres of farmland.

I blew a .23 and was carted off to jail. It was one of those small, Andy Griffith ass jails where they only had four cells. Kush had a similar incident a few hours before, and with us being the only two inmates there, we chopped it up and exchanged information. That was a year prior. Our relationship since then grew exponentially. We did everything from hustling, to fucking hoes together, to doing music. What I liked about him was he was an avid chess player that gave me a run for my money every time we played. It was hard to find an evenly matched opponent, but I found that in my guy Kush Krinkle. He was a cool, laid-back, activist, who organized a hell of a protest.

I looked over at my homeboy as he weaved the police SUV in and out of traffic, dodging pedestrians and the objects that were being hurled at us. The windshield was cracked, and all of the windows were busted out, but we were still riding that bitch.

"We're gonna have to go on foot until we can get to the van where the bikes are," Kush said as he pulled to a stop.

There was a Black Lives Matter utility van being guarded by our team outside of Briva Health on East Lake Street. Kush stashed the bank bags in a hidden compartment in the van.

Me and Queen grabbed a couple of Schwinn Mountain bikes, and Kush hopped on a pretty ass all-red Apollo 110cc Dirt Bike.

"King, Gabe is under the bridge. Stop and see him, then join me up top," Kush said before kickstarting the bike and zooming off.

"You ready for this ma?"

Queen held her head high and replied, "As ready as I'll ever be!"

I nodded, got on the bike and pedaled toward Hiawatha Ave. There was a gray tent with BLACK LIVES MATTER spray-painted on it underneath the bridge. This, too, was surrounded by team members that I recognized. Queen and I parked our bikes and went in. It was hot and muggy, and Gabe was sitting down Indian style, sweating bullets and working various devices.

"Hey, King, Queen. Y'all alright?" Gabe asked while he typed on his MacBook.

"Yeah, we're good, man. I lost my earpiece though," I said.

He reached into a duffle bag and dug me out a new one. "Here you go, bro."

"Good lookin' man. Can you give me the rundown at what we're looking at before we join Kush on the bridge?"

Gabe nodded. "Ok, here's the deal. All law enforcement, including the National Guard, have been dispatched to the bridge. There are no more than 1,000 of *them,* so obviously the numbers are in **our** favor. They are prepared for the standoff. They have been deploying tear gas, flash-grenades, and rubber bullets to keep us from moving forward. There's a tote full of gas masks outside of this tent. Make sure you guys each grab one before you go. You're gonna need them."

"I've already been tased. I'm glad y'all plugged me with this special fabric," I said. My protest gear was made out of Thor Shield, a polyester fabric bonded to a conducted material that neutralizes the electricity coming from nonlethal electricity weapons. Stun guns, batons, tasers and the like had no effect against my Thor Shield.

"I'm glad too. The police are going to use every tactic shy of lethal force to try and control the streets. King, you're gonna be front and center, so be careful. You too, Queen. They have already showed us that they don't care about our protest, so prepare to be targeted once you step up to the plate."

"Alright Gabe, thanks man," I said and shook his hand. "Keep me posted on any new details you find out," I told him as we exited the tent.

"Will do, King. Give them hell. bro!"

You gon' be my baby
Love me, love you crazy
Tell me if you with it
Baby come and get it
Maybe try a new thing
And let's spark a new flame

I looked at Queen, whose Chris Brown ringtone was going off as we hopped on our bikes.

"Shit, I've gotta take this real quick," Queen said. "Hello? Hey, baby. Yeah, I'm fine. I really am in the middle of some serious shit right now. No, no, daddy I'm OK. I probably won't be sleeping tonight, but I'll call you whenever I'm sitting still for a minute. Kk. Love you too." Queen hung up and looked at me. "Sorry."

"Hey, it's all good. I didn't know you had a man."

"Yeah..." She trailed off and looked at her phone.

"He ain't down for the cause?" I asked, referring to his absence.

"Umm, he's kind of four-thousand miles away," Queen said as we pedaled up the street.

"Say whaaaa?"

"Yeah, he lives in Hawaii."

"Damn, that's far as a muthafucka."

"I know it is, but we make it work," Queen replied.

I dropped the subject as we rode up to the crowd carrying fire torches and signs. "Let's do this," I said and got off my bike. We walked our bikes through the crowd that seemed to part for us as we made our way to the front.

"No justice, no peace!" I shouted to the SWAT team that stood on the bridge. I coughed in the thick, yellow smoke from the tear gas that surrounded me. Fire, smoke, and signs of all kinds were in the air. It was time to put on my gas mask.

Kush and a team of young goons rode dirt bikes and motor-cycles back and forth along the bridge. There was a wall of smoke wafting from the concrete that divided us from the police, who were fifty yards away. They stood in riot gear holding 40mm Tactical launchers and shields to protect themselves from the objects we threw at them.

I was in the heart of the protests, where outrage and sorrow were the only emotions in the air. 12 didn't give a fuck about us, and we were letting them and the world know we weren't about to give a fuck about *nothing*!

I looked around and saw people holding bullhorns and poles.

It was 2020, and the scene looked like something from the civil rights movements in the 60's. The only thing missing was the water hose. Even the fires couldn't be contained, because there were so many blazes raging. One of their own kneeled on a defenseless black man's neck for eight minutes and thought it was justifiable. We were *heated*.

"Fuck 12!"

"Hell no, we won't go!"

"Black lives matter!" "Fuck the police!"

"No justice, no peace!" thousands of people shouted at the line of police in heavy tactical gear. Their shielded helmets and Kevlar vests took everything we threw at them. Rocks, bottles, flash-bangs, and Molotov cocktails were hurled from the side that wanted justice. Tear gas, rubber bullets, and mace were used by the side that wanted order.

I was in all black and in panther mode. I watched as protestors were grabbed like ragdolls and thrown to the ground by the National Guard. Reporters and civilians captured the live footage of police brutality against peaceful protestors. When I saw their cowardly acts, it enraged me. Both sides heaped gasoline on to the fire, and shit exploded something vicious!

Me and my boys stepped up to the wall of National Guard officers and yelled at the top of our lungs. "Fuck youuuuuuu!" the gas mask muffled my voice, but my tone was clear and precise. I pointed in the face of my oppressor.

He was as still as a statue. His hand gripped his baton tighter the more I screamed. My finger touched the plastic shield on his helmet, and I was shoved by two officers at once.

"Get your muthafuckin hands off him!" Queen shouted as she thrust the phone in the cops faces. They pushed her too.

"Get back ma'am!"

"No you didn't just put your muthafuckin' hands on me!" Queen yelled in outrage.

"Hold up, ma. I got this," I motioned for her to step back as I pulled a smoke bomb from my backpack quickly and swiftly. I threw it and knocked one of the officers helmet off. **POOF!** It exploded on contact, spraying streams of smoke all over. I took a few steps back as the officers blindly swung their batons at me.

"Fuck the police!" I yelled and threw another one. There was so much smoke, I couldn't see five feet in front of me. The smoke didn't stop the rubber bullets they shot at us.

This went on for several minutes. Us throwing shit at them and them shooting tear gas and rubber bullets at us.

"King, the choppers are coming to your location. Be warned, the choppers are arriving soon," Gabe said into my earpiece. "They are going to release some kind of liquid agent to disperse the crowd. Keep covered."

"Thanks Gabe, I will." I heard the approaching helicopters in the near distance. I turned my back to the police and raised my bullhorn. "When the helicopters come, use your signs to cover your heads," I told my people.

"Bitch ass police! Y'all ain't shit," Queen said as she waved a middle finger at them.

Kush rolled up to me. "It's about to get ugly fam, but I'm here witchu," he said and laid several mortar tubes that were fused together on the ground. When he lit them, we all stepped back and watched the multi-shot aerial fireworks propel in the sky. The variety of explosions in different colors and patterns shot three-hundred feet in the sky. It was the only beautiful sight in the midst of such an ugly situation.

All of that changed when the helicopters arrived. "You all have five minutes to clear this bridge, or we will be forced to evacuate it as we see fit," a voice from up above said. The only voice I listened to from the sky was God's, and that wasn't Him talking.

I raised my middle fingers to the helicopters and shouted, "No justice!"

"No peeeeeeace!" Everyone else said in unison.

"You have two minutes to evacuate. I repeat, in two minutes we will clear this bridge."

"Hell, no, we won't go! Hell, no, we won't go!" I began the chant that thousands of people repeated with me.

"You've been warned," the voice above said, and the trap doors on the bottom of the helicopters opened up. Clear liquid rained down on the crowd.

"Ahhhhh!" people screamed when they realized the helicopters above us were dumping gallons of acid on them. Neither side wanted to budge, but that all changed in a heartbeat.

The only thing that turns people into track stars, are bullets.

Rrrrarr! Rrrrarr! Rrrrarr! The unmistakable sound of gunshots rang out, and people scattered in all directions. I looked around to see which direction the shots were coming from, and what I saw shocked me. An armored truck was barreling towards us with a lone man on top of the hood firing a machine gun.

"Run! Run!" Someone shouted, and that was what we all did.

The barrage of gunfire parted the crowd like the red sea. The National Guard returned fire with a vengeance. I heard screams like someone got hit, but I didn't stop to see who it was. I got the hell out of dodge.

Men and women ran in all directions, ducking bullets, and trying not to get trampled in the stampede that ensued. I held Queen's hand and ran like the wind. I noticed people climbing down a sheet that hung off the side of the bridge. We left our bikes behind and climbed down the sheet to safety. I went first so I could catch her when she came down. She was scared to let go and make the twenty-foot jump to the street.

"I gotchu, ma. Come on," I said, holding my arms out. She took a deep breath and jumped. She screamed all the way down, but I caught her.

"You're OK babygirl. Let's go."

It was pure chaos in the streets. Flashbangs went off. Molotov cocktails flew in the sky like shooting stars, and the smoke was thick in the air. The Lake Street Midtown Metro Station was fairly empty, so we took cover in there. I did a quick sweep to see who was inside. A few of my team members were there waiting for transportation.

"There's supposed to be a bus coming for us," a dude named Pee-Wee said.

"Let me know when it's here. We'll be in the office," I told him.

I took Queen to the small office in the back that was completely ruined. I sat on the floor, put my back against the wall, and took my black Timberland boots off. Queen captured our sanctuary on her phone before she sat down next to me. I got some bottled waters out of my backpack, and we sipped from them in silence. She took me completely off guard when she grabbed my legs and put my feet in her lap.

"You're a brave man, King. I've gotta give it to you," Queen said as she began massaging my sore feet. "You were great out there."

"Thanks ma, so were you."

"Thank you," she said and smiled.

"Uh, I know my feet stankin' right about now. You sure you wanna be doing that?"

Queen sniffed the air. "Yeah. They stink alright, but it's ok. You deserve your feet rubbed after what you've been through."

I couldn't disagree with her on that one. I kicked back and let her do her thang. "Don't think I'm returning the favor though," I joked.

"Damn, a Queen keeps a King from being checkmated and can't even get no reciprocation?"

"Nah, I'm not like that. I'll rub your corns and bunions."

"Fool, I don't have corns *or* bunions. My feet are pretty, thank you very much!"

"Mmmmhm. Yo' toes probably look like Cheetos," I said and laughed.

"You know what?" Queen pushed my feet off her lap. "Massage your own damn feet."

"Awww, come on now, ma. You know I was just playing."

"I don't care. You ruined the moment."

"Oh, did I?"

"Mhm," Queen said and stood up. "I gotta check on my girl." She pulled her phone out and made a call. When no one answered, she hung up and made another one.

I fired up a blunt while she spoke to her dude.

"Hey bae. Yeah, I'm ok. Huh? I don't know. My voice is going hoarse from all the yelling I've been doing... Uh, me and a friend are waiting on our ride now. At the Bus station... yeah. Yes, baby. It's been a hectic night, boo. I'm tired and sore, and I desperately need my feet rubbed," Queen shot daggers at me when she said that.

I smiled and patted the ground next to me.

"I'm not sure Koa, but I will let you know when I find out."

When Queen sat next to me, I put her feet in my lap. I took off her black Air Force Ones and removed her socks. I scrunched up my nose and fanned my face. She held the phone away from her and hit me in the shoulder.

"Boy, quit playing. My feet don't stank," she whispered to me.

Queen was right about two things. One, her feet did *not* stink, and two, she had some of the prettiest feet I'd ever seen. I wasn't really a feet kind of guy, but I do appreciate a woman who keeps her shit looking right. Queen had a fresh pedicure with glossy French tip nails that were on fleek.

"Huh? Oh I... mmmm, yes, baby," Queen moaned. She may have been talking to her dude, but it was *my* hands that were making her feel good. She had her head against the wall and her eyes closed as my fingers worked their magic. "Koa, I know, daddy. You gotta stop... mmmm, worrying. I'm, uhhhhh, I'm a big girl... Baby, Jenny's calling me on the other line. I gotta answer this. OK, I will. Uh-huh. Uh-huh. Love you too," Queen said and hung up with him.

"Jenny, girl, where you at? Whaaaa? For real? Well, damn... Shit, me and King at the Midtown Station. Uh-huh. Mutha-fuckas supposed to be coming to get us any minute now. I don't know. Just meet us back at Kush's crib, or do you need us to come scoop you? Uh-huh. She is? Where you find her at? For real? Dang, that's crazy. Yeah, you can bring her with you. I didn't even know she was out here. Yeah, that's cool. Alright, girl. See you later. Be safe. I will. Love you." Queen hung up and sighed.

"Everything ok?" I asked.

"Ehh, kinda sorta," she responded.

"What's wrong?"

"Nothing I can't handle. Dang, share the wealth my nigga," she said and reached her hand out. I passed her the blunt, which she grabbed and took a long pull, then coughed immediately.

I laughed lightly. "Easy, easy now. This dat killa shit," I said, taking the blunt from her.

"I... I don't smoke that... often." She gasped in between coughs.

"Hmpf. You sure as hell was high as a kite the first time *we* met."

"Um, no I wasn't. I had just gotten off work," Queen said.

"Uh, I'm pretty sure you weren't working that night."

"King, what are you talking about?"

"What am I talking about? Girl, what is you talking about?"

"I'm talking about when I met you at the store and you gave me your books. Remember my co-worker was giving you shit? Speaking of which, her crazy ass is here. My homegirl ran into her at one of the stores she looted."

"Oh yeah?"

"Yup. I didn't take her for the protesting type, but even she's fed up with the bullshit."

"Damn, you really don't remember me, huh? You and your girl got some serious amnesia."

"King, again, what are you talking about boy?"

I stood up and stretched. I hit the blunt and let smoke tendrils waft from my nostrils. "You don't remember the men you get intimate with?"

"Intimate? King —"

"New Year's Eve, Queen. I'm the nigga that ate your pussy until... " I trailed off.

Queen gasped in horror and stood up. "Oh... my... God —"

"Becky... look... at her... *butt,*" I said and chuckled.

❦ 14 ❦
QUEEN

W hen the shock and horror of what I found out sunk in, I went on the defense. "Shut up, King. That shit ain't funny."

"Nah, it ain't funny, but you know what is? You not knowing this whole time that I'm the nigga you was getting it in with on New Year's Eve! Shaking my damn head."

"Look, you had dreads then, didn't you?" I asked with my hand on my hip. He was pissing me off, making it seem like I was some kind of hoe bitch who fucked random dudes and didn't remember them. Yeah, I was fucked up that night. Shit, it was New Year's Eve, but he wasn't about to confiscate *my* crown just because I was too intoxicated to remember him.

"Yeah, I had dreads, but my face is still the same. All these tattoos were on my skin then —"

"Look, my bad for not remembering you. I —"

"Ha! Your bad? Yeah, it's your bad alright. Your alien pussy gave me nightmares for months! And on some real shit, I ain't ate no pussy since you. And I used to *love* eating pussy."

"Look muthafucka, I ain't got no alien pussy. I had a cyst that needed to be removed. I'm sorry that you had to go through that. I didn't know it was there. I sure as hell wouldn't have let you go down on me if I did," I told him seriously.

"Yeaaaaah right. You bitches will knowingly be on your period, have an STD, or an eggplant cyst and *still* have a mutha-fucka all up in your pussy," King said.

"Nigga, you got me fucked up! I don't know what kinda bitches you be fucking with, but I don't get down like that," I said, getting heated.

"Whatever you say, Queen."

"Nigga, fuck you."

"Nah, I'm good. I don't fuck alien pussy ma."

I picked up a handful of debris and threw it at him.

"Watch it now. I don't hit women, but I got some homegirls that'll get in your ass."

"Bring it! I wish a bitch would step to me. I'll knock her ass out cold," I said.

"Mhm. Yo' hands ain't better than the hood bitches that I know."

"Nigga, try me and find out for yourself. And you better bring ten or mo' of them hoes to fuck in my business. Me and my girl Jenny will put all them hoes on they back!" Our argument was bringing the hood back out of me. I'd come a long way since my days on 12th and Locust, but the sheer embarrassment from not knowing I'd hooked up with King was setting me off.

"Well, don't be throwing shit at me, and you won't have to worry about my homegirls."

"Whatever, King. I'm not worried about no bitch **or** no nigga."

"Yeah, a'ight lady. I —" King got a call and stopped mid-sentence. "Talk to me, fam. OK. Yup, we're still here. A'ight, we're coming out now." He disconnected and looked at me. "They're about to pull up soon. Let's go."

I folded my arms across my chest and sulked out of the office. Pee-Wee was waiting for us.

"The bus is coming, y'all," he said.

"Yeah, I just got the call. Everybody ready to roll?" King asked.

The few people that were part of our team all nodded and gathered their belongings. When I heard the loud, constant honking, I knew it was Kush driving the bus. When I stepped outside, I looked both ways. Up and down the streets, buildings were engulfed in flames. King must've read my mind.

"It looks like we're in hell," he commented and got on the bus.

I sat in the first seat and asked Kush, "What's next?"

"I'm scooping up everyone I can get to, and then we're going back to my crib," Kush told me. I nodded and sat back in my seat. I could see the bank bags overflowing with money on the floor next to him. I was quiet as I got lost in my own thoughts. My mind was racing all over the place. Luckily for me, I had one hell of a distraction before my eyes.

I stared out the window as we cruised through the city. It looked like we were in a fucking Hollywood film. We literally went to war with the police. Thousands of people roamed the streets protesting. Fires burned like the devil's playground. Rioting and looting were rampant. Everything was going down. I was really feeling some type of way. Death and destruction were all around me. My boyfriend was a million miles away, and all I wanted was for him to hold me and tell me everything would be alright. I'd just found out a man I'd spent hours defending was a man I once almost had sex with and didn't even know it.

I was extremely relieved when we finally got back to Kush's crib and saw that Jenny was already there.

"Giiiirl, am I glad to see you," she said when she saw me.

"I know, right," I responded and hugged her.

"Queeeeen!" Heather gushed and hugged me. "Fancy seeing you here."

"*Me?* Heather, never in a million years would I have guessed you'd be here protesting."

"Why on earth would you think that? You're not my only

black friend. *Queen.* Plus, I dated a black guy once when I was in college," Heather said. *Yeah right. I bet he was as black as Carlton from the Fresh Prince was,* I thought to myself. She went to Harvard, so I knew any "brothers" there, were definitely more Tiger Woods than Kevin Gates. Her comments validated what I felt about her stance on the protests. Since we worked together, I kept my mouth closed.

"Well, I'm happy you're here to support the Black Lives Matter movement Heather."

"Thank you. I was surprised to see Jenny —"

"Girl, please," Jenny interrupted her. "I'm the one that was surprised to see your ass looting."

"Heather!" I said in shock.

"Whaaat? I like free stuff too, ya know," Heather responded.

"She sho' do. Bitch was in the Walgreens trying to get all the pills out the pharmacy."

We all laughed. Anyone who knew Heather knew how fond of the "Skittles" she was.

Heather shrugged. "Hey, I don't need hygiene products and clothes, but I do need *drugs!*"

"Did someone say drugs?" King said, holding up a bag of weed as when he entered the room we were in. I smacked my lips and picked up my phone.

"Ayyyyy!" Jenny said excitedly and raised her hands. "We were just talking about mind-altering substances."

We all laughed at Jenny's choice of words. Even she knew she sounded ridiculous.

"What chu waiting for nigga, roll that shit up!"

"Uhh, I'm the one supplying the weed. *You* roll it up," King said and threw the bag of weed in Jenny's lap. "Or are you one of those females that smoke blunts but can't roll'em?"

"Shiiiid, gimme some blunts, and I'll show you how a bitch roll. My blunts probably better than yours, fool."

"OK, OK. We'll see about that." King opened a pack of

Swisher Sweets and gave Jenny one. "You roll one, and I'll roll one."

"Deal," Jenny said as she began busting the cigar down.

"Well, I won't pretend like I know how to roll one of those things. When I smoke pot, it's usually out of pipes or bongs," Heather commented.

"I figured that," King said to her.

"What does that mean?" Heather asked gullibly.

"Never mind ma. Don't worry about it."

"Oh, OK. Hi, I'm Heather," she extended her hand.

"I know. We've met before," King said and shook her hand lightly.

"We have?"

"Heather, do you remember the guy who gave me those books at the store?" I jumped in.

"Wait, that's you?" she said with an open mouth.

"Yeah, that's me. Damn, what's with y'all three? None of you muthafuckas even remember a nigga?" King shook his head in disgust.

"King —"

He put a hand up to silence me. "Don't worry 'bout it, ma. Yo, my blunt's done. So, since *you're* still rolling, we'll fire this one up and compare them when you ready."

"You can't rush perfection," Jenny replied as she licked the brown wrap and twisted it.

"I got this from the gas station. Didn't think they'd have my team up here," King held up a Milwaukee Brewers lighter. It had their famous M on it. "Queen, do you mind recording me blaze up? I want to capture my first time using this."

"What for? It's just a lighter," I responded.

King shook his head. "Never mind. I can do it myself." He grabbed his phone.

"No, I'll do it for you, King," Heather said. "Here, give it to me. I'll do it."

I looked upside Heather's head. She was acting nicer and

more weird than usual. It was probably the painkillers she just jacked from Walgreen's. The bitch was loopy as fuck.

"Kiiiiing," Heather sang. "Wow, you really have a beautiful name."

I rolled my eyes.

"Thank you. And you have a beautiful face," King replied and handed her the phone. I smacked my lips and rolled my eyes again. Heather didn't say anything. She just smiled and blushed.

"Alright, you two. You're making me gag with this mushy shit," I said, feeling a bit salty by their flirtatious communication.

"For real, for real. Fire that shit up or give me the lighter so I can show you how my blunt smokes better than yours," Jenny said.

"Whatever. Let me see that," King took Jenny's blunt and inspected it. "Not bad. It looks pretty good."

Jenny took her blunt and his Milwaukee Brewers lighter out of his hands. "I know it does. Now let me spark this muthafucka since you're playing in your ass!" We all laughed while Jenny lit the blunt and blew a cloud of smoke in King's face. "Yeeeeah, that's it right there."

King took his lighter back and motioned for Heather to start recording. She got up and sat right next to him. King spoke directly to the camera. "Yeah, this is the wind down to a legendary night. Swwwww." He inhaled and blew smoke rings in my direction. I fanned my face. King twisted his fingers together, making an M, then he held the lighter up. "From the Miltown to Minneapolis, we in this bitch!"

"Hell yeah! We in this bitch!" Jenny joined in, throwing her own M's up to the camera.

Since I was on King's right side, I was the first person he passed the blunt to.

"Nah, I'm good." I declined it.

"Oh, now you good? You was just smoking with me when you was rubbing my feet," he said, trying to bust me out.

"Oooooh, what was y'all on?" Jenny inquired.

"Nothing!" we shouted in unison.

"Not a damn thang," King said.

"Mmmmhm. Something was poppin' if Queen was rubbing your feet."

"Jenny, just drop it. I did the man a favor cuz he was on his feet in them big, dumb ass boots all night," I said.

"Alright, girl, my bad. I know you ain't do nothin' bad cuz you wit Koa."

"Koa? Is that the dude you was talking to while you were massaging my feet?" King smiled.

If looks could kill, the glare I gave him would've had him six feet under right then and there.

"Queen!" Jenny gasped in shock.

"King, you can go on with that bullshit. Jenny, let me talk to you for a second." I got up and walked out. Jenny closed the door behind her and joined me in the hallway.

"Queen, tell me you wasn't rubbing that nigga's feet while you were talking to Koa?"

"It's not what it sounds like," I protested.

"Shiiiiid, it's pretty cut and dry." She paused to hit the blunt. "You either did or didn't."

"OK, OK. I did. But when I talked to Koa, it was *King* who was rubbing *my* feet."

"Oooh, girl. You're nasty!"

"Don't go there with me, Jenny. We didn't do nothing."

"Mmmmhm, if you say so. Y'all the ones massaging each other's feet in the middle of a riot and shit. But hey, your secret is safe with me."

I waved her off. "Whatever, bitch. Do you know where we know King from? He was one of them niggas at the Sybaris with us."

"From New Year's?" Jenny asked incredulously.

I nodded my head. "Yeah, he had dreads then, and uhhh... I trailed off.

"Uhhh what?"

"He was the one eating my pussy that night."

"Shut the fuck up! That was him?"

"Yup. I didn't know it 'til a little bit ago. That's when shit changed between us. We were good up until then."

"Damn, Queen, that's crazy."

"You're telling me. I feel so fucking stupid ya know?"

"Girl, don't feel bad. You was fucked up that night."

"Yeah, but still..."

"Still what? He had dreads then. Even *I* don't recognize him."

"I know, but he said some shit that made me feel pretty low. Like I was a hoe bitch that fucked plenty dudes and never remembered them or something."

"But you know you're not like that Queen."

"I know. But then I'm letting this nigga rub my feet while I talk to my man... I don't know... I just feel guilty, ya know?"

"Look, a massage is just that. Would it be any different if you went to a professional masseuse? Of course not. Don't let that nigga get to you. He probably salty cuz he wanna fuck you and he know you ain't going," Jenny assured me. No sooner than she said that, we both heard the unmistakable moans of pleasure and ecstasy coming from inside the bedroom. I shook my head and asked Jenny for the blunt. It was gonna be a long night.

✵ 15 ✵

KING

"Suck my dick you nasty ass white bitch! Yeah, choke on dat black dick you filthy, little slut. Mmmmm!" I said between gritted teeth. I was palming the back of Heather's head, trying to ram my dick through the back of her neck! She gurgled, choked, and gagged happily. Her passionate and slutty enthusiasm was why niggas like me got down with bitches like her. They were nasty and didn't give a fuck... just like me.

I remembered the snooty bitch from the store and how she hurled insult after insult at me. *A nigga write jail letters, huh?* The bitch thought she was funny, but I knew what she was on. Blowing a nigga off because she really wanted to ***blow*** a nigga. Classic "Brat syndrome."

In the BDSM world, a brat is someone who wants to be put in their place by a dominant figure. They want to be "punished" for acting bratty, showing out, and behaving naughtily. That was something most women enjoyed, being disciplined for being a "bad girl." Be it ass slaps, hair-pulling, pelvis pounding, being choked, or some form of brutal, hardcore sex, it was something they get off on. The rougher, the better for them. In reality, they were trying to intertwine pain and pleasure because those two always brought out the most-intense emotions and feelings, and that's what a lot of people craved. They want to *feel*.

When I saw the look on her face and heard the tone in her voice when she complimented my name, I knew I could fuck her. I read women very well. Her whole demeanor oozed sex. Even though I had just helped tear the city up and bring it to 12, I was still full of pent-up aggression. It was only right that I took it out on a white bitch.

Heather was one of those in-shape, svelte women. She stood 5'10" with long legs and even longer hair. "Yes! Pull my fucking hair!" she shouted while I pounded her pussy from the back.

"You like that shit, don't chu, bitch?" I leaned forward and growled in her ear.

"Oh God, yes. I... fucking... love it!"

I was able to wrap her long, brown hair around my wrist three times. I held her silky tresses in my fist and yanked her head back damn near by her roots while I fucked her relentlessly.

"Fuck yeah! Gimme that big... black... cock! Ooooh, King. Yes, baby, yessss."

I knew Queen and Jenny were outside listening because I could see their shadows moving around beneath the gap under the door.

I'm not gonna lie, ol' girl had some *great* pussy. It was tight and super-duper wet. Every time she came, a thick, white cream coated my dick and sent chills down my spine.

"Whose pussy is this? Huh, bitch? Whose muthafuckin' pussy is it?" I shouted loud enough for even the downstairs people to hear.

"Oh, God, King! It's *your* pussy!"

"Yeah, I know it. Who's your Daddy?"

"You're my Daddy King. Oh my God! Oh my God! Fuck me Daddy!"

I flipped Heather on her back and put her legs on my shoulders. She was one of those flexible ass Pilates chicks, so I was able to twist her in all sorts of ways. I long stroked her and we both watched my dick go in and out of her repeatedly.

"God, you have a beautiful cock," she breathed. "Choke me, Daddy. I want to cum on a King's cock while being choked."

She didn't have to tell me twice. My hands went around her flushed neck, and I squeezed. The smile that spread on her face was priceless. Instead, I wasn't seeing her. I was seeing Derek Chauvin and every racist cop I'd ever encountered. I gritted my teeth and took my anger, hate, and rage out on Heather's body.

I squeezed her neck until snot bubbles came out of her nose and she began foaming at the mouth. I was killing her softly, but she didn't give a fuck.

"Yeeeah... that's it. Mmmmhm." She wheezed.

My pelvis slammed down on hers with all my might. The loud echo of skin slapping against skin ricocheted around the room and turned us both on even more. I knew what she wanted, and she knew how I was feeling.

"Punish my naughty white pussy. Fuck it, pound it, stretch it." Heather was one of the most vocal, freakiest women I'd banged up until then. Her dirty talk made my orgasm bubble to the surface like a sleeping Volcano.

"Ohhhhhh shiiiiiiiit!" I yelled and pulled out of her sopping-wet cunt.

"Yeah baby, cum on my face. Give me all of that superior cum," she demanded and stuck her tongue out.

My first blast splashed on the headboard. After that, I emptied a pint's worth of cum all over her sweaty, red face and tits. I painted her white body with my white nut, then I collapsed next to her, and like a good little slut, she licked me clean.

"Damn, your friend has some good pussy," I said to Queen when I walked into the hallway.

"Fuck you, King," she shot back.

I laughed. "Nah, I'd rather fuck your girl Heather. She got

that wet wet. And the only eggplant in her pussy is the one I just put in her!"

Queen lunged at me, but Jenny grabbed her. "Leave it alone, Queen," Jenny told her.

"I hope y'all enjoyed the show," I called over my back as I went into the bathroom. I took a piss, washed my dick off, and checked my text messages. By the time I grabbed a soda from the refrigerator, all hell had broken loose.

I ran to the bedroom where all the commotion was happening.

"You punk ass bitch! You ain't shit," Queen screamed while holding Heather by her hair.

They pulled each other's hair and rolled around in the bed. Heather was still naked, and Jenny was standing against the wall watching.

"What the fuck, yo?" I said.

Jenny shrugged. "Let 'em fight. Shiiiiid."

"Fight" wasn't the word I'd use to describe what happened. Queen punched Heather in the stomach, which caused her to release Queen's hair. It was *on* then.

"You wanna get your pussy beat up by a black man? Well, you're about to get your *ass* beat by a black *woman!*" Queen shouted and three-pieced her. One punch to each eye, and then one to the nose. She hit her so hard that blood shot out of her nostrils like a cannon. "I'll be damned if you make a fool of me. This is... the last... time... you —"

"Alright, Queen, get off her, ma," I said as I grabbed her and pulled her off her co-worker.

"Get your fucking hands off me, King! You ain't shit," she said as she shrugged me off. The tears that ran down her face confused me. *Why the fuck was she so emotional? Didn't she have a man? Why did she care that I banged the white bitch?* I thought to myself.

"Come on, Queen. Let's get some air," Jenny said and

escorted Queen outside. I looked at Heather who was sprawled out across the bed, naked, crying and bleeding all over.

"Crazy fucking bitch. What's her problem?" Heather said and spat blood on the floor.

I shook my head and went to have a word with Ms. Queen.

※

"I NEED TO SPEAK WITH YOU," I SAID TO QUEEN. HER AND Jenny were in the backyard drinking from a Crown Royal bottle.

"King, now is not the time," Jenny said as she stepped in between us.

"Naw, it's cool. Let's hear what this dog ass nigga has to say," Queen said.

"Damn, where is all this hostility coming from? A few hours ago, we were just the black Bonnie and Clyde. Now I'm all sorts of dog ass niggas and shit? Damn, what the fuck, yo?!"

"Yeah, cuz you been acting real foul and disrespectful." Queen chugged from the bottle and wiped her mouth with the back of her hand. She'd gotten really buzzed in such a short amount of time. She was slurring her words and cussing like a sailor.

"Queen, I don't care how you feel about me. You were in the wrong for beating up on that poor girl," I told her.

"Poor girl?" Queen scoffed. "Nigga, please. Fuck that hoe. Nasty ass bitch! She *been* had an ass whoopin' coming. She'll be a'ight when the swelling go down."

I shook my head and looked around the backyard. There were people congregating around a bonfire and our heated conversation was becoming quite the spectacle. I knew Kush kept a motorcycle in the garage, so I went and got it.

"Come on. We're going for a ride," I said and revved up the crotch rocket.

"Nigga, I ain't going no damn where with you," Queen announced defiantly.

I got off the motorcycle and picked her up by her underarms. She kicked and squirmed but I didn't care.

"Damn, fool, at least let me grab a few things to take with me," she said.

I put her down and she went around front. She came back a couple minutes later with a small bag. I placed it inside the seat and sat her on the red Ducati Monster before I got on myself. I put her hands around my waist and sped off.

"Hold on!" I shouted back at her. She rested her face on my back and tightly wrapped her arms around my stomach. I smiled and headed for Powderhorn Park. I zig-zagged through pedestrian traffic, trying not to hit anyone. The streets were still alive and filled with people. A crescent moon played peek-a-boo behind all of the black smoke that filled the air. There were even more buildings on fire than before. Minneapolis would reap the consequences of that racist killer cop for years to come.

When we got to the park, I hid the motorcycle in a bunch of bushes so no one would walk off with fam's shit. There were lots of tents in Powderhorn because it was known as a main location for the homeless. That didn't faze me though. I knew it was a peaceful place where a muthafucka could go and get their thoughts together. I spent many nights walking the park, smoking weed, and brainstorming ideas.

Me and Queen walked to the Powderhorn Lake and sat on an embankment. The fires burning throughout the city could be seen from our vantage point.

"So why did you bring me out here? Are you gonna kill me, then rape my warm corpse?"

I raised my eyebrow. "Damn, ma. What the fuck did I do to you to make you switch up like this on me?"

Queen opened the bag she brought with her. She pulled a bottle of Crown Royal out and twisted the cap off. After she took a few sips, she looked at me and said, "You disrespected me, King. I've been nothing but good to you since we've met."

I cleared my throat and raised one eyebrow.

"Okaaaay. So our first encounter was awkward. And I sincerely apologize for not realizing that me and you were together on New Year's Eve. I was gone out of my mind. It was the first time I tried Molly —"

"You popped a roller?"

"Yeah. Why do you think I got so freaky with your ass?" Queen said, and we laughed. "But on some real shit, King, that comment you made about all bitches fucking with dudes knowing they're on their rag, or got an STD, or got an *eggplant* in they pussy was bogus. I'm not that kind of bitch, King, for real. I'm a Queen," she said and raised her head up high.

"OK, OK, my bad. You're right, ma. I was out of line. I apologize. I have no filter, so I go a little too hard for people sometimes.

"Hey, I get it. You're the ultimate alpha male, but until you get to *know* me, please don't judge me or put me in the category with other bitches."

"You sound like my homegirl Meesha," I told her.

I looked at her face as the moon shined down and illuminated her beauty. I'm a firm believer in everything happening for a reason. What was God telling me?

❧ 16 ❧

QUEEN

"A Queen must have her crown," I said and raised the bottle in the air.

"Quit stealing my slogan and hand me that bottle, witcho stingy ass," King retorted.

"*Your* saying? Boy, please. I been drinking Crown since before you was born," I said.

"Whatever," he said and laughed. "How old is you? Twenty-five, twenty-six?"

I blushed. "You're too kind. Shit, I wish I was still in my twenties. I'm thirty-four."

"Dammmmn, for real? You look good as hell for mid-thirties."

"Thank you. How old are you? Forty-five, forty-six?" I said and smiled.

"Oh OK, you got jokes, huh? A'ight then."

"Boy, shut up. How old are you?"

"Thirty-seven."

I nodded my head and passed him the bottle. "Here, since you're old enough to drink." He sipped from the bottle while I pulled my portable chessboard out. "You play?"

His eyebrows shot up. "Hell yeah I do!"

"Good, let's get it in then," I replied.

"Bet!" King said and began setting up the pieces.

"We'll see what your chess game is like. I was hoping you could play, and if you didn't, I was gonna teach your ass. You can't be named King and not know how to play this game."

"Oh, I know how to play alright. It's a thinking man's game, so —"

I cleared my throat. "Um?"

"Oh, my bad, it's a thinking *person's* game." He corrected himself.

"Sexist muthafucka you," I said and we both laughed. "So, who is Meesha?"

"She's my best friend. We been riding tough for ten years now."

"For real? That's what's up. So your best friend is a female?"

"Yup."

"You don't see that too often nowadays," I commented.

King was setting up his pieces. "Somebody spit a pill out on your board, and you forgot to wipe it off?" he said as he rubbed a yellow mark that stained my chessboard.

"Is that another shot at me over my first time popping a pill?"

"Nah, I was just... never mind, your move," he said moving his Knight first.

"Ohhh, OK, you're coming out swinging," I replied and moved my pawn.

"So you really a Crown Royal fan?"

"Hell yeah. My mama used to drink that shit, that's before they had a hundred flavors!"

King laughed. "I know, right? I don't know why they haven't made a grape flavor and a watermelon flavor yet."

"Uh, so their company can be boycotted as being racist?" I said with a raised eyebrow.

"Well, damn, it's not really racist if the consumers are

requesting it. And it ain't no secret that us black folks love grape and watermelon."

"Not me, I don't like grape-flavored stuff."

"What about watermelon?"

I was silent but nodded my head.

"Mhm, I knew it. Yo' ass would guzzle down some watermelon Crown," King said.

I didn't deny it, because I know he was right. "Check."

"What the... "

"Yeah, muthafucka, let me see you get your ass out of this one." I bragged.

"I'm a strategist... out of check."

He made a good move that prevented me from checking him without losing one of my major pieces. He was one of those players that planned three moves ahead because I calculated where he went every time. He was smart, but I was smarter.

"Sooooo, is everything, um, alright down there?" King asked me.

I looked at him with a stern look on my face.

"Whaaaat? I'm just asking. I ain't never seen no shit like that."

"Yeah, I'm OK. It was a benign cyst. They removed it, and everything worked out."

"Well, that's good."

"Yeah. Besides a yeast infection from having sex on the beach, my pussy has been A-1 since our incident."

"Ugh, you went from eggplant alien pussy to doughy pussy?" King joked.

However, it was me who got the last laugh. "Boy, shut up. Checkmate!"

"What the? ... How did you? ... " King was at a loss for words.

I shrugged and smiled. "Best out of five. Spin the board."

I DIDN'T KNOW IF HIS GAME WAS STRONGER, OR IF HE JUST thrived from having his back against the ropes, (I believe it might be the latter), but I beat him the first two games, and after that, he turned into a beast and beat me three straight.

"Great comeback." I complimented him.

"Why, thank you. Bet you thought you had me after I went down 0-2, didn't you?"

"Yeah, I'm not gonna lie. I thought I was gonna glove you," I said, referring to the term when you beat an opponent five straight games.

"Glove me? Ha! You funny as hell. I ain't been gloved since I learned how to play."

We put the Chessboard up and walked around the baseball field talking, smoking, and drinking. Despite our petty beef, I genuinely liked King. I was into his literature from the first page I read, and I told him that.

"So, where's my money? I gave you those books, and you never sent me any compensation."

"I was meaning to, and I wanted to buy your others as well. It's just, shit, I've been crazy busy, and this Corona shit has my mind in an uproar!" I admitted.

"I feel you on that."

"But I gotchu. You really are a talented writer, King."

"Thank you, Queen. I just write whatever comes from my crazy imagination."

"I'll say! *Our Future World* was the wildest, most-creative concept I've ever read. I could see things turning out like that the way we're headed."

"I know, right? Look around. We're going to hell in a handbasket."

"Shiiiiid, bullshit ain't nothin' my nigga. *You* might be going to hell in a handbasket, but *I'm* going to Heaven in a Hot Air Ballon!"

"Is that right?" he asked and smiled.

"It is."

"I admire your confidence in your faith," he told me.

"Thank you. It's something I believe firmly in. People will always let you down, but if you're God's child, He'll *always* have your back."

"Amen!"

"So, what are your plans after this?"

"Well, once shit settles here, I'm going back to Wisconsin to push my books and collect my settlement money from my old job. Then I can open some businesses and put some talented people on," King said.

I nodded in agreement. "That's what's up."

"What about you?" he asked.

"I don't know. All this shit has really made me think."

"What chu mean? Another brother getting killed by the police?"

"Well, yeah. This whole outcome really. I mean, look what we just did tonight. We fucking made the police run from their own headquarters," I said and laughed.

King laughed too. "I know. Man, that shit was wiiiiiild. I've never seen nothing like it."

"Me neither, but witnessing it up close and personal has made me want to be a part of the movement on a consistent basis. Not just when another one of us gets killed, ya know?"

"Yeah, I know what you mean. So what is it you want to do?" King asked me.

"I'm not sure what my role will be, but I'll contribute on the regular from now on."

"That's what's up. What do you do for a living right now?"

"I work in nursing."

"Oh yeah?"

"Yeah."

"That's what's up. You seem like the care-giving, nursing type," King said.

"Why do you say that?"

King shrugged. "I don't know. It's just your presence. You

have that helping people aura about you that most people in your field possess."

"Yeah, well I do like to help others in need."

"Cool, cool." King nodded. And Jenny's your bestfriend?"

"Yup. That's my ride-or-die bitch right there!"

King laughed. "She's from the hood like a muthafucka."

"Sho' is. 12th and Locust."

"Wait, y'all from the Mil?"

"Yes sir. Born and raised," I told him.

"A'ight then. 39th Vliet is my stomping grounds."

"Ohhhh, OK. I could tell by your swag that you were from Milwaukee."

"Yeah, I love my city, but I moved up north to get away from the bullshit," King said.

"I know what you mean. I ain't gotta worry about drive-bys or some street punk trying to rob me up here."

"Queen, you ain't never lied. I done had to demonstrate on a few muthafuckas back home. I'm not with the black-on-black violence, but if a nigga try me, I'm gon' give him what he asking for."

"Shiiiiid, you're not wrong."

"I'm not with the game-playing and fuckery these clowns out here be on these days."

I nodded and we sat in silence for a few minutes collecting our own thoughts.

17

KING

"This world is never gonna be the same ya know? We're going to be wearing face masks until we die."

"God, I hope not. That shit is annoying and uncomfortable as fuck!" Queen replied.

"Man, all this shit is crazy. Them people done made a disease and unleashed it on us. I really think we in Revelations."

"You know what? I was thinking the same way not too long ago," Queen said.

"Shiiiid, that's why I live my life to the fullest and do what I can *today* because I don't know what's gonna happen tomorrow," I admitted.

"Hey, I get it. This is my first time protesting and going all out like we did today, but it felt great! I just want to leave my mark in some kind of way. Get my voice heard."

"As you should. Shit, as we *all* should. I try to do that through my writing, but it only reaches so many people. And most of my stuff is just fun entertainment —"

"*Our Future World* is more than just entertainment though. That is one deep, thought-provoking book right there," Queen said.

"Thanks. It was my first time going in that direction. I wanted to do something different."

"I can't wait to read the other ones. What's the new one you wrote?"

"*A King Must Have...* It's a motivational book with a humorous twist for those down and out. I was going to write a spin-off —"

"A Queen Must Have?"

"You know it, baby," I said and smiled.

"Ooooh, now that is something I'd want."

"How about you help me write it."

"King, I'm no writer."

"Yeah, but you are a Queen, aren't you?"

"Hell yeah, nigga."

"A'ight then. You can help me structure it so that it's tailor-made for the women. Because even though I can empathize and put myself in other people's shoes, only a woman — well, a *Queen*, can truly express her feelings and desires in a way that I can't."

"That's true, but I wouldn't know what to do," Queen said.

"Well, I'll ask you questions, and you'll give me your unbiased female opinion. And we'll chop it up and kick it throughout the writing process so I can use your vibe as the theme."

"Wow, are you serious?"

"Yes, I am."

"Well, fuck it, why not? Count me in!" Queen said and high-fived me.

"You're cute."

"Huh? Shut up, boy. Tell me more about you? Who is King?"

"Who am I? I'm that nigga!" I said and laughed as Queen rolled her eyes. "Naw, but for real though, I'm a hustler that just wants to live comfortably and put my team on."

Queen nodded her head. "You got any brothers and sisters?"

"Nope. You?"

"I had a brother, but he died a few years ago," Queen said with sadness in her voice.

"Damn, I'm sorry to hear that, ma."

"Yeah, some nigga killed him over a no-good bitch my brother was fucking."

"Psssh, another brother killed over a punk ass bitch!" I shook my head in disgust. "And people wonder why I feel the way I do towards females."

"And how is that?"

"Bitches ain't shit," I replied and shrugged

"Hmpf, whatever."

"It's true. Most females have no heart, no morals, and no direction."

"Is that why you treat women the way you do?"

"Look, I treat a muthafucka the way they deserve to be treated. If they a punk bitch, I'm gonna treat them like a punk bitch. If they're good people, then they get the royal treatment."

"And since you're a first-class asshole, is that how I should treat you?" Queen said.

"Why I gotta be all that? You still mad cuz I fucked your friend?"

"You were bogus for that, King."

"Why? You're not my woman. And don't you have a man? Why are you so concerned with who I have sex with?"

"King, I don't give a fuck who you have sex with!"

"Obviously you do if you're salty about —"

"You're right. It's none of my business, so just change the subject," Queen said.

"So, when is your birthday?"

"August 23rd."

"Awww shit, Virgo in the houuuuuuse! Wait, isn't that the same day as... "

"Kobe Bryant? Yup."

"Cool. R.I.P Kobe."

"It's so crazy what happened to him."

"I know, right?" I said and shook my head.

"When is your birthday, King?"

"August 14th.

"Ahhh, you're a Leo. That explains a lot," Queen remarked.

"What's that supposed to mean?"

"Nothing. So, what cha gonna do for your birthday?"

"I was thinking about throwing a face-mask-themed birthday party."

"Oh, OK. That sounds dope."

"Yeah, I was gonna have a cash prize giveaway for the three best masks to make it fun."

"Heyyy, that's a good idea, King."

"Yeah, maybe we can throw a joint party since our shit is so close together."

Queen nodded her head. "We might be able to do that. I haven't made any plans yet."

"Well, let me know if you want to do something. 2020 done put a monkey wrench in a lot of shit, so my original plans to go to Costa Rica is over. But I'll be damned if I don't celebrate my birthday in style!"

"That's what's up. I even know what I'm getting you."

"Oh yeah?"

"Yup. Some manners!"

"Psssh, whatever. I have plenty of manners, thank you very much."

"Mhm," Queen groaned.

"Look, ma, I'll be honest with you. I fucked your friend for two reasons."

"King, I don't —"

"Naw, naw, hear me out now. For *one*, I fucked your friend to piss you off. I was salty that none of you muthafuckas remembered me, especially you, so I had a score to settle in those regards. And for *two*, I was gonna treat her punk ass real rough if she was gonna give up the pussy, which she did. Bitch thought I wouldn't remember how she insulted me when I first met her? I made sure I gave her the bidness and that y'all heard it!"

"So you fucked her to hurt me?"

"Eh, I didn't want to hurt you, cuz you really shouldn't be hurt seeing that you have a man. But I did want to get a reaction out of you, which I did."

"That's childish, King. You're too old to be playing those kinds of games."

"I ain't playing no games. I'm just doing me."

"If you say so," Queen said and rolled her eyes.

Queen was acting like she was Ms. Perfect and shit. I wanted to ask her why she let me massage her feet while she talked to her boyfriend on the phone but knew she'd throw a fit.

"So, are you and your homegirl Jenny roommates?"

"No, we have our own places. I live by myself in a comfy lil' two-bedroom. You?"

"I have a couple of cribs here and there. I'm trying to move to Cali someday though."

"Oh yeah?"

"Yeah, I need to be in the entertainment industry. Book, movies, music, fashion, I'm trying to get into all of that," I told her excitedly.

"You're very ambitious, King. And your talent speaks volumes. You can definitely make it."

"I think so too. I just need my shot." We sat in silence for a bit more, getting lost in our own thoughts. "What about you? What do you want, Queen?"

"I want a Queen cave," she replied.

"A what?"

"Don't chu got a man cave?"

I thought about that for a minute and smiled. I decided to hit her with the real. "I have a black S&M Dungeon if that counts as a man cave."

Queens eyebrows shot up, and then she smiled. "Psssh, whatever boy. I'm for real."

"I am too, but never mind all that. Tell me what your Queen cave's gonna look like."

Her face lit up, and the sparkle in her eyes when she described her vision was priceless.

"Everything is gonna be baby blue. The furniture, the walls, the mink carpeting —"

"Mink?" I cut her off. *What did she know about mink?*

"Yeah nigga, a Queen's feet must walk on only the finest," she said and winked at me. "I'll have the big screen on the wall, the wrap-around leather sofa, and a quality sound system in the walls."

I was intrigued as she described her safe haven. I had to admit, that muhfucka sounded dope!

"There will be a pool table at the far end of the cave by the mini-bar. And you know *all* flavors of Crown will be chilled. A few Arcade games will sit against the wall."

I had to see what her taste in games would be. "Which games?"

"Duh, the classics. Ms. Pac-Man, Donkey Kong, and Mario Kart," Queen said.

"Um, you had me with the first two, but Mario Kart?"

"Yeah, boy. That shit fun as hell. You ain't never go-karted before?"

I felt nostalgic thinking about the times I went to Bonanza Go-Kart park with my moms and then my mood flipped.

"Yo, fuck all that. Mortal Kombat, NBA Jam, Pac-Man, and Mike Tyson Punch-Out are the games on my cave's wall!"

"Ugh, you would have the violent games. Such a typical man."

"Why the fuck you think they call it a man cave? We cave *men*. Club a muthfucka over the head, drag 'em in the cave, grunt, beat our chest, and leave 'em to rot while we go hunt for our food. And when we want to be animalistic in *other* ways, we'll throw the old lady over our shoulders and go dig out **her** cave."

Queen bust out laughing. "Boy, you silly!"

"Shit, I'm for real. But I wanna hear more about your joint. Or was that all?"

"Hell naw, that ain't all. Man, I got a baby-blue throne in front of the TV. A dressing room, the laundry room —"

"You live in yo mama basement, don't you? That's where this cave is, isn't it?" He smirked.

Queen punched my arm. "Shut the fuck up, King. *No*, I don't live in my mama's basement. But my Queen cave will be in the basement of *my* home."

"OK, OK, I'm feeling that."

"Yeah, and I'm gon' have acres of land that I own. Miles and miles of green where I can plant vegetables and have the garden of all gardens."

"Again, you had me at miles of green, but after that? Ehhh."

"Fuck you, King. I like to garden. Getting my hands dirty is worth seeing my hard work grow into something delicious," Queen stated.

"Damn, that's deep, ma. I like that," I admitted.

"You're an artist, so you can appreciate someone expressing themselves with their hands in positive ways."

I nodded my head. "So let me guess, you want to buy a home in the country with plenty of acres for your royal garden —"

"Check!"

"A baby blue Queen cave dripped out —"

"Check! And don't forget about my she-shed."

"She-shed?" I asked, raising my eyebrow.

"Yeah, I'm gonna have horses I can ride. *All* females, hence, the she-shed."

"Damn, that's sexist. You ain't gon' have no stallions in that muhfucka?"

"Hell naw. Why? So they can try to fuck on everything?"

"Hey, that's what studs do." I shrugged.

"Anyway, my she-shed got an underground bunker in case the world ends."

"Shiid, we better get there now, cuz this might be it," I said and looked at the sky. Flames and smoke danced in the distance sky as chaos of all kind unfolded in Minneapolis.

"Well, I ain't got the crib yet, so we gonna have to find somebody farm and take over that muthafucka!"

Checkmate. "Oh yeah? You hit one police over the head and whoop one square white bitch, now you miss gangsta chick huh?"

"Nah, boo, I ain't no gangsta chick. But I know we're in ride or die times right now. Look at this shit." Queen pointed in front of us.

From where we were, we could see dozens of businesses on fire. There weren't enough Firefighters to battle the blazes. It looked like hell on earth. *Could this be the end?*

"Is this not the craziest year of your life? I mean, you probably seen some shit in the streets, but ain't nobody seen the shit we done been through this year."

"Queen, you definitely got that right," I said and shook my head. I was hoping to wake up one day to find out this has all been a dream, but the blood dripping down my face was letting me know this wasn't no dream. I got hit with debris at some point during the riots and wrapped it up with some gauze and medical tape.

"King, you're gonna need stitches cuz the blood has seeped through the bandage." Queen leaned over me and took the sopping-red dressing off my forehead.

"Well, you're da nurse. Stitch me up and get me right," I said and laid on the grass.

"Um, I'm not really a nurse though."

"What chu mean? Didn't you say you worked in nursing?" I asked, confused.

"Nursing home. I'm a CNA. I take care of the elderly. Feed them, bathe them —"

"Wipe their ass?"

Queen laughed. "Yeah, it's my least favorite part of the job, but yes, I wipe their butts."

"That's cool. I got love for everybody in the medical field. Everyone has a job that *someone* has to do."

"Yeah, I wish I could do more in my job though." Queen sighed.

"How so? Don't you love what you do? If you don't, it's time for a new profession."

"King, don't get me wrong, I love helping those that can't help themselves, but I really want to be a nurse."

"OK, so what's stopping you?" I asked.

"NCLEX."

"Incest?"

"No, fool. NCLEX. It's the test you have to pass to become a nurse."

"Ohhh OK, you had a problem passing it?"

"Yes. I had, have, and will always have a problem with NCLEX. It's my kryptonite."

"Just get a tutor. You'll —"

"King, I've had tutors. I've had nurses at the top of their classes try and help. I've... shit, I've done everything I could possibly do. NCLEX is impossible."

"It can't be impossible if other muthafuckas done passed it. Come on now, Queen, I don't even know you like that, but I'm sure you're a smart woman. You have a brain. And you still owe me some brain," I said and had a flashback to the eggplant situation.

"Boy, shut your nasty self up!"

"On some real shit though, do you love what you do, Queen?"

"Mmm, I used to. I mean, there are some days I feel rewarded when I help someone or have a drama-free day, but then I have those days where I'm swamped and dealing with the bullshit from management and their corporate strife. I get shit on so much, *literally*, that I can say *no*, I do not enjoy my job."

"Damn. You need to talk to my girl Meesha. She's a Life Coach and really good at what she does. I think she can help you."

"Oh, OK. Yeah gimme her number, and I'll definitely hit her up. I think it's time for a career change. I definitely want to do something different with my life. I just don't know what."

"Yeah, I feel you. A lot of people don't know what they want to do with their life. Many of us just ride the waves on our journey to finding out our true purposes in life."

"You said that in your book," Queen said.

"I did. And it's true. How about kids? You have any?"

"No. I want to be established before I bring a child into this unstable world."

"I agree 100% with you. I'm the same way. That's why I ain't got none.

"Boy, please, as big of a player as you are, you're trying to tell me you don't have any kids?"

"Nope, not a one. There were some miscarriages in the past, but nah, there's no Prince or Princess for this King yet. And to be honest, I don't know if I'll ever find a woman good enough to birth my seed."

"Well, that's better than spreading your seed to everybody and they mama."

"Yeah, I was taught responsibility from an early age, so I'm ahead of my time and cut from a different cloth than these niggas out here with twenty different babymamas," I remarked.

She looked at me and nodded her head. I may have rubbed her the wrong way by some of my remarks, but I saw nothing but respect in her eyes when I expressed my feelings openly and honestly.

❧ 18 ❧

QUEEN

The travel ban and curfew had put a serious damper in all aspects of my life. I had only seen Koa once since February. All the summer events from Concerts, Fairs, Shows, Amusement Parks, and any other thing that involved groups of people, was cancelled. Had it not been for King, my Summer would have been extremely boring.

Once the George Floyd thing died down, we returned to our everyday lives. Heather and I were no longer on speaking turns after our fight, but I didn't give a fuck. I really never liked the snooty bitch anyway. I even went so far as encouraging King to take her finances, which he happily did. He even broke bread with me a few times.

When his settlement came in, I helped him line up a couple of his business ventures. His BFF, Meesha, had become my go-to person I confided in because she was not only a great listener, but she also gave *great* advice.

Everyone always commented that King and I would one day be together just because of our names alone. We ignored the allegations though. We were friends. I had a man, he had many of women, and that was that. Even though we got closer and closer the more we hung out, I wasn't trying to cross that platonic line.

"Happy Birthday to youuuuuu... " the crowd of 100 sang to us.

Me and King decided to collaborate and throw a joint birthday party. We returned to our hometown of Milwaukee, WI and rented out a banquet hall. We chose a royal and face-mask theme.

King was the big Baller, so he was the one who splurged on the party. There was a stage where two thrones sat. A baby blue one for me, and a royal blue one for him. There were two-hundred pre-rolled blunts in a dispenser, which guests helped themselves too. Sexy men and women (that me and King hand-picked), were dressed in royal attire as they walked around half-naked serving guests shots of Crown Royal.

DJ Keefe Trotter was playing all the jams that kept people dancing and having a good time. YFN Lucci and Boosie Badazz were going to perform ten songs later in the evening and I was really looking forward to that.

Me and King blew out the candles on our massive cake that was shaped like a castle.

"Yayyyyy!" People clapped, took pictures, and cheered.

"Before I cut the cake, I want to make a toast," King said as raised his iced-out pimp chalice cup in the air. "This year has been fucked up, but we're still in this bitch. Here's to persever-ance and better days."

"Perseverance and better days!" The crowd announced and clinked glasses with one another. I looked around at the men and women attending our bash. Most of them, I knew. The facemasks made it hard to tell who was who, but I was already picking out my favorite candidates for best face-mask. $100 was going to the first-place winner. $50 to the runner-up, and $20 for third-place. I was buzzed as fuck and feeling good. The photographer asked me and King to go onstage so she could take our pictures. I straightened my crown, smoothed out my dress, and hooked my arm through King's before we walked on stage.

He was very handsome in his three-piece suit and blinged-out crown. His face mask had tiny crowns with colorful rhinestones on it. He was drippin' sauce like a motherfucker! We took solo pictures in different poses and on our respective thrones. Then we took group pictures with each other and our friends.

"Hey, Traci," King called out to the photographer. "Can you get a couple of us on our thrones together?" King said. He sat me in my comfy, baby-blue chair, then sat in my lap.

I laughed at him while he made faces and posed for the camera. I joined in the fun, sticking my tongue out and crossing my eyes.

When he got up and sat in his chair, I followed suit by sitting in his lap. We repeated our goofy antics but all of that ceased when Koa walked in. We looked at each other, but the looks in our eyes were different. I was surprised yet happy to see him. He, however, was quite upset by what he saw when he entered my birthday bash.

"Why the fuck are you sitting on that motherfucker's lap?" Koa asked.

"Well, happy to see you too," I responded.

"Happy birthday, Queen. Looks like you're having fun without me."

"Koa, you said you wouldn't be able to make it. I'm glad you did though." I wrapped my arms around his neck and kissed him.

"Well, I wanted to surprise you. Plus, you deserve birthday sex on your special day."

"Ooooh, so you came 4,000 miles for this pussy, huh?" I said with a smile.

Koa put his hand underneath my dress. "I sure did. It's *my* pussy," he said, but he was looking over my shoulder. I turned around to see King smiling at us.

"Yeah Daddy, it's your pussy. I'm so glad you came. Come on, let me introduce you to my friends." I grabbed his arm and showed him off to all my girls. A lot of women brag on their man but the dude don't be about shit. I actually had a real-life gentleman that I was proud of. I saved the last introduction because I didn't know how it would go.

"King, this is my boyfriend, Koa. Koa, this is King," I said. The two men sized each other up and shook hands.

"You got a good woman here, man," King said.

"Yeah, I know. This is my boo," Koa said and put his arm around my shoulder.

"Well, glad you could make it, bruh. Enjoy the party," King said and walked off.

Looking back on it now, it was kind of my fault for getting Koa so shit-faced. I wanted to have hot, dirty, sex, and I knew if he was fucked-up, he'd give me exactly what I wanted. We downed shot after shot of Crown Royal until our words were slurring and we were stumbling into people.

"I forgot your gifts in the car babe. I'm gonna go get them and be right back," Koa said.

"I'll go with you, hun. Now that you're here, I don't want to leave your side." I grabbed his hand, and we walked to the parking lot where King and a few of his guys were on their knees shooting dice on the pavement.

"That's just Ghetto," Koa remarked loudly as we walked past them.

I didn't think anyone heard him, but King did. "What chu say, dog?"

Koa looked back but didn't respond. I pulled on his arm so we could get to the car. I wanted to see what he got me. He popped the trunk and handed me two gift bags while he carried two gift- wrapped boxes himself.

"You got something you wanna get off your chest my guy?" King said.

"Excuse me? You talking to me?" Koa replied on the defense.

"Koa, come on. King, be cool," I pleaded.

"I am cool. Your man's the one mumbling shit under his breath. Speak up, nigga!"

"Listen, brother, I suggest you refrain from calling me the N-word." Koa said. That caused a bout of laughter from the men shooting dice, including King.

"Square ass nigga. You better fall the fuck back! This is my party muthafucka. She may have invited your square ass but —"

"King!" I shouted.

"A'ight ma. I'll be cool. But you need to check your dude. Don't be coming to my muthafuckin' party with all that hate and hostility," King replied.

"It's all good, King. We're going back inside," I said. "Come on, bae."

"No, Queen. This, this, *thug* needs to learn some respect." Koa let my arm go and stepped to King.

I got right in the middle of them. "Come on guys. It's my birthday party. King, it's yours too. This should be a drama-free event. Put y'all ego to the side and just be cool, alright?" I pleaded with them both.

Koa looked at me with reason and went inside the building.

"King, are you gonna be cool?"

"Yeah, ma, long as your dude stays away from me," he said and returned to his dice game.

"Koa, I haven't seen you in months, and you show up causing a scene?"

"I'm not causing a scene. But I don't like that guy." Koa informed me while we walked down the hallway.

"Like him? You don't even know him!"

"I don't have to know him well enough to know that he's Ghetto trash, and I don't care for him. I don't even know why you're hanging around people like him, Queen."

"Because he's a good friend to me. He's talented, motivational, and has a big heart."

"Is that why you were sitting on his lap when I walked in?"

"Koa, is that what this about? We were just taking pictures
—"

"Well, let me take a picture with some female in my lap and
see how you like it. Matter of fact, tell Jenny to sit in my lap, so
we can get a few pics together." Koa was beginning to slur his
words and stumble when he walked.

"You know what? I'm not even gonna respond to that. You
wanna take pictures with my friends? Go ahead I'm not trippin'.
You wanna get in your feelings cuz I took some pictures with the
person I'm having this party with? That's your problem. But ain't
nothing going on between me and King. We're friends, and that's
it," I told him.

"Mhm, whatever, Queen," Koa remarked and walked off from
me. I smacked my lips, put my hands on my hips, and turned
back around. I was drunk, mad, and feeling some type of way.

✺ 19 ✺

MEESHA

Queen had just declared her love for King and told him she'd leave her dude for him. King, being who he was, shattered her hopes and dreams. He called me first and broke the news to me.

"Shorty talking about she love a nigga and shit. Can you believe that?" he said.

I didn't want to tell him that yes, I could believe it. I just listened to him vent.

"Ya see that shit? Bitches always throwing monkey wrenches in the game. Fucking up a nigga head and shit. Why a muhfucka can't just be cool? Why bitches always gotta be catching feelings?" Usually, when a female wanted to be more than friends, he didn't react that way, but since it was Queen, he was showing his true emotions.

"King, didn't you tell that girl that she was the perfect woman? That God couldn't have built a greater creature?" I reminded him.

"Yeah, but we'll never work."

"How come?" I asked.

He couldn't tell me a logical answer. He was scared of getting his heart broken again. His defense mechanism was to self-sabotage love because it was easier to not be in love than to suffer from a broken heart.

Shortly after I spoke with King, Queen called me. She was bawling her eyes out and asked if she could come over to talk.

"Queen, it's not you, it's *him*. You have to know King to know why he does what he does."

"I just don't get it, Meesha. He says I'm the woman of his dreams, but when I give him the greenlight, he puts on his brakes. What the fuck?"

"Do you know why, girl?" I asked her. I wasn't going to get in the middle of it, but the girl was so distraught, and King was wilding out as of late because he was an emotional wreck.

"No, Meesha, I don't."

"Girl, that nigga got trust issues with women that runs deep," I told her.

"I mean, I know that. The *Trust Nobody* tattoo on his neck told me he had trust issues. But we've been riding pretty hard together, doing everything. I've showed him the type of ride or die friend I am *and* the kind of woman I am to my man. Why isn't that enough?"

"Girl, get that wine out the fridge and two glasses. I'm about to light this blunt up and I'm gonna give you a better understanding of our friend King." I grabbed the lighter and sparked up the Tropical Fusion Swisher Sweet full of Purple Passion Fruit weed. Queen came back with the Barefoot Pink Moscato and poured two big girl glasses for us.

"You already know we once had a thing. Once I found out he was somewhat of a dog with commitment issues, I kicked his ass to the curb. But we had so much fun when we were together that I missed his ass like a muhfucka. All of our common interests always brought us to the same places —clubs, movies, restaurants, concerts. No matter where I was, whether I was on a date or with friends, I seemed to always run into King. I used to think the nigga was following me." I laughed and passed Queen the blunt.

"Girrrrrl, you know I don't be smoking like that, but I'll hit it a few times," Queen said before toking on the blunt and coughing.

"Yeah, I know you don't, but you need to be relaxed to swallow this shit I'm about to hit you with."

Queen looked at me with a worried look on her face. She hit the blunt hard and passed it to me.

"So how did y'all just keep it in the friend zone?"

"The same way you have. Y'all ain't fucked yet... right Queen? Queen?"

She was biting her lip and looking at the floor.

"You sneaky bitch!"

"Whaaaa? We didn't have sex. We just... "

"You just what, Queen?"

"Well, he ate my pussy when we first met, but... "

"But what?" I was on the edge of my seat hitting the blunt hard. King didn't tell me he went down on Queen. He told me about all of his exploits.

"Well, he came to our party at the Sybaris on New Year's and —"

"Wait, wait, wait! Are *you* eggplant bitch?"

"Huh?"

"Eggplant bitch. He said he started getting freaky with a chick at the Sybaris, when all of a sudden a big purple thing popped out her pussy, and he got the hell out of there." By the way she hung her head in silence, I knew it was her. King never told me her name. He just referred to her as "Eggplant Bitch" with the "Alien Pussy."

"It was a Bartholin's cyst," Queen said quietly.

"A Bart Simpson clit?"

"No, hoe. A Bartholin's cyst!"

"What the fuck is that?" I asked, wrinkling up my nose and blowing smoke out my nostrils.

"One of those unfortunate things women get sometimes," Queen said.

"Damn, did that shit hurt?"

"Well, according to the doctor, I should have been in a lot more pain. It was more like a constant ache. I thought my pussy was telling me I needed some dick cuz it had been so long. But it turns out, I had something growing inside my vajay-jay."

"Damn, Queen, so *you're* eggplant bitch... " I laughed hard and loud.

"Shut up, Meesha. That shit ain't funny."

"I know, I know... My bad, Queen. I... I just didn't know. That's crazy though," I said.

"You're telling me! There was no rhyme or reason for me getting one either. It was just one of those female things we get plagued with."

"It's cuz Eve ate that damn apple. That bitch is the reason behind all our pain. Childbirth, Aunt Flow, PMS —"

"And Bart Simpson clits!" Queen said, and we laughed.

"I know, right?" I high-fived her. "Men are so lucky. They ain't gotta go through the shit we do. They can pee wherever they want —"

"Do whatever they want, and not get judged for it —"

"Say whatever the fuck they want and *still* become President-"

"Meesha, don't even get me started on Cheeto man's sexist, racist ass."

"Yeah, we ain't even gonna go there," I said and finished my glass of wine. I refilled both of our glasses, and we got back to the subject at hand.

"Meesha, keep that shit 100, are you and King friends with benefits? You can tell me. I won't say nothing."

"Shiid, ain't nothing to tell. Me and King haven't done anything sexual in eight years. He's like a brother to me, so we just keep it platonic. Yeah, he slaps my ass from time to time, and we crack dirty jokes, but that's as far as it goes."

"I see the chemistry you two have. People see y'all out and think you're a couple. *I* thought you two were together. Y'all finish each other sentences and have this magnetic chemistry that's so... I don't know... it's just a beautiful thing to see."

"Aww, well, thank you ma. It is kinda crazy. We're so in tune and so on the same page with a lot of stuff. And hey, I love the man with every ounce of my being. It's not easy, but King is a good dude. I don't believe in some of his behavior or the things he practices, but he has the right to his own beliefs and opinions. He broke certain things down to me that helped explain and show why he is the way he is."

"Things like what, Meesha?"

I sighed heavily as I contemplated whether to tell her or not.

"Did he ever tell you why he has sex with the best friends of the women he dates?" I asked, and she shook her head while sipping more wine.

"His first ever three girlfriends cheated on him with his homeboys. So ever since he was a teenager, he's had this *Bitches Ain't Shit* mantra because of them."

"Wow. I didn't know that," Queen said and shook her head.

"Yeah. He knows kids will be kids, and he tried to chalk it up to just being young, dumb, and full of cum. But just as he was changing his philosophy, thanks to a woman twice his senior, she died in a car accident and turned his world upside down."

"Oh no, that's horrible!" Queen exclaimed, holding her hands to her mouth.

"I know, right? In King's mind, every woman who has ever meant anything to him has hurt or abandoned him in one way or another. So he has this bulletproof wall that he puts up that keeps him from getting too emotionally attached."

"His ten percent keepsake you mean?" Queen asked.

"Yup."

King says no matter who a person is, the most he'd EVER trust them was ninety percent because he would always reserve 10% that no one could obtain in case they let him down. That "ten percent keepsake," as he calls it, would keep him from going over the deep end if someone he trusted were to ever shit on him. In a way, I understood his philosophy. If you gave someone 100% of your trust and they broke it, one would naturally be devastated. But holding back even a little bit of trust, could help a person get over the betrayal and disappointment in a way that wouldn't leave them stagnant.

"King learned from an early age that women were heart-breakers who abandoned and hurt him. You can't tell nobody I told you this, and if he found out, he'd kill me, so promise me you won't utter a word of what I'm about to say to you," I told her seriously.

She was a good woman, and we were becoming good friends, so I felt she should know why the man she belonged with wasn't going to be the man of her dreams.

"I promise. I won't tell a soul," Queen put her hand on the Bible sitting on my coffee table and raised her right hand.

I sighed and took a sip of wine. "When King was eight-years-old, his mother dropped him on a relative's doorstep and ran away with some man who didn't like kids."

"Oh my God, that's terrible," Queen said in shock.

"I know, right? If the woman who gave him life could leave him for another man, what would *other* women do to him?"

"Damn, that's fucked up. She really just abandoned him like that?"

"Yeah. He didn't hear or see her until his 18th Birthday, when she showed up at his party like she hadn't just disappeared from the face of the earth for ten motherfucking years."

"Are you serious, Meesha?"

"As a heart attack, Queen. King has deep emotional and psychological issues behind the abandonment of his mother. I paid for counseling some years back after he revealed that to me, but he thinks shrinks are full of shit hacks."

"He would." Queen snorted, knowing all too well just how stubborn King was.

"I went to a lot of sessions with him for support, but it just wasn't his thing. He did learn to open up more because of it though. Before counseling, he was so standoffish and... *mean*. Like, he had a deep hatred towards women for a long time."

"I think you loving him so genuinely changed that," Queen commented.

"I'd like to believe so. I've shown him that not all women are alike. Just like all men aren't alike. But he's dealt with so many shady ass bitches that he can't help but see women a certain way. You coming along has helped change his perspective too," I told her. Since kicking it with Queen, King has matured greatly. I knew it was because he was catching feelings for her, and I told him so.

"Boy, you need to stop running from love and actually try a real relationship for once," I would tell him, but he wasn't trying to hear that.

"Well, thank you," Queen smiled. "That man knows how I am. I've risked my life and freedom for him several times —"

"Oh, he knows you're a ride or die. He tells me all the time." I laughed, thinking of all their crazy adventures over a few months span.

They were in two riots, and an ex that she put in prison got out because of the Coronavirus and stalked her. King was forced to deal with him, and together, he and Queen buried Jamal's body in the woods somewhere.

"Well, if I'm so ride or die and beautiful, then why the hell won't he get with me?"

"Did King ever tell you how he got into the BDSM Dom shit?" I asked. When she shook her head, I told her about the cougar who opened up the kink world to him.

"Whoa! Let me guess, she cheated on him with one of his friends?"

"Nope... she died in a car accident. Drunk driver killed her," I revealed.

"What?"

"Yeah, the woman twice his senior I told you about? That was her," I said.

"Holy shit, Meesha. For real?"

"Yup."

"So *that's* why he snapped on me for driving drunk."

"Oh yeah. He will go the *fuck* off if he knows you been drinking and want to drive. He loved that lady and holds her in a special place in his heart," I said.

Queen sat in silence and processed the information she was given. I was sure a lot of things made more sense once I clarified some stuff for her. She'd only known King a few months and had already been through a great deal with him, but we've been through ten years' worth of shit.

"I need to hit that blunt please," Queen said, extending her arm, and I passed it to her.

"King has it in his mind that whoever he loves or whoever loves him, eventually, will leave him. So far, I'm the only one who has lasted as long as I did. He always jokes I that I been rocking with him longer than his own moms, which is true and really, really, sad when you think about it. His mom had him until he was eight, then dumped him off. I have been with him for ten plus years, and I would *never* throw him away."

"Damn, I don't even know what to say."

"Nothing you can say really. All you can do is continue to be there for him and hope that he sees that you two are soulmates," I told her.

Queen gasped. "Meesha, do you really think we're soulmates?"

"Your name is Queen. His name is King. What chu think?"

"Just because our names are linked doesn't mean anything."

"Mhm. Look, girl, me and King may not have worked out, but trust me, I've been waiting for that one that was perfect for him, and guess what? *You're* her."

"Well, tell him that cuz he sure doesn't seem to think so," Queen huffed.

"Oh, he thinks so, and he *knows* so. He's just fighting it."

"Stubborn muthafucka," Queen spat.

"Girl, what man *isn't* stubborn?" I said matter-of-factly.

"I know, right? Like damn, if they just listen to us, this world would be a much better place."

"He'll come around though. You're the first person to penetrate his wall of defense —"

"You mean that bulletproof glass he has surrounding his heart?"

"He can be cold at times, but now that you know what you know, can you blame him? Just keep being you. Give him time. He'll change his mind."

"So should I break it off with Koa to show King I don't want him anymore?"

"Queen, don't hold on to something you don't want just for the sake of it. It's not fair to the other person, and it's a waste of time on your part," I told her.

"Yeah, you're right. It's just crazy. Koa is the fairytale guy. He wants to move me to Hawaii and get married and have a family...
"

"Oh yeah?" I asked.

"Yup, but I don't want that white picket fence life though. I want —"

We been on a tragedy for months,
why can't you agree with me for once?
Maybe we can be on chill tonight....

My ringtone interrupted Queens thoughts. "Hello? Yes, this is she... " What I was told made me drop the phone as I sat there with my mouth open and an ocean in my eyes.

"Meesha, Meesha what's wrong girl?"

"It's the um, Medical examiner. King was pulled over by the police. He was shot twelve times. He's... " I froze in shock. I didn't want to believe what I was just told.

Queen grabbed my shoulders and shook me. "Meesha, he's what? Talk to me Meesha!"

Tears ran down my face in streams of pain. "Queen, they killed him... King's dead."

AUTHOR'S NOTES

We all want that happy ending, but as you know, we don't always get what we want. Too many of our black brothers are dying from senseless violence. By the hands of each other, *and* the police. We saw how a young white kid could walk down the street in the middle of a riot with an Assault Rifle and not even get *approached* by the law. Had that been a black kid, he would've been shot from all directions by every cop on that street. So yeah, it's sad to say, but racism is still alive and thriving in 2020.

The devil won't stop until we're extinct. If it's not bullets, it's Cancer. If it's not Cancer, it's helicopter crashes and drunk driving fatalities. Death is imminent and comes in many forms. All we can do is live our life to the fullest and try to better ourselves each day.

While King and Queen are *fictional* characters, there are a lot of real-life situations these two have been through that a lot of people have done or can relate to. And no, I am not King lol, but I can relate to the character that I created in many ways.

There is some King and Queen in all of us. How you represent your crown will be your legacy.

This is my 3rd Urban Novel with many more books and projects to come.

Fan mail and special requests may be sent to:

Perk Thirty
    P.O. Box 1954
    Eau Claire, WI 54703

CPSIA information can be obtained
at www.ICGtesting.com
Printed in the USA
LVHW031753171220
674449LV00003B/538